W9-CUL-817

# A Meeting of Minds

# A Meeting of Minds

by Carol Matas and Perry Nodelman

Simon & Schuster Books for Young Readers

SIMON & SCHUSTER BOOKS FOR YOUNG READERS
An imprint of Simon & Schuster Children's Publishing Division
1230 Avenue of the Americas, New York, New York 10020

Text copyright © 1999 by Carol Matas and Perry Nodelman
All rights reserved including the right of
reproduction in whole or in part in any form.

SIMON & SCHUSTER BOOKS FOR YOUNG READERS
is a trademark of Simon & Schuster.
Book design by Jennifer Reyes

The text for this book is set in Goudy.
Printed and bound in the United States of America
10 9 8 7 6 5 4 3 2 1

Library of Congress Cataloging-in-Publication Data

Matas, Carol, 1949-
A meeting of minds / by Carol Matas and Perry Nodelman.
p.    cm.
Summary: When Lenora and Coren find themselves trapped in a world
created as part of the contest held in preparation for their marriage,
they encounter the writers who are responsible for their existence.
ISBN 0-689-81947-1
[1. Psychic ability Fiction. 2. Fantasy.] I. Nodelman, Perry. II. Title.
PZ7.M423964Me 1999        [Fic]—dc21        99-12239

FIRST
EDITION

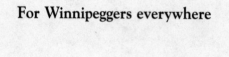
For Winnipeggers everywhere

# A Meeting of Minds

Chapter 1

Lenora's hands flew to her cheeks. It felt like a thousand ants were biting her face. But it couldn't be ants—not right in the middle of the freshly cleaned and renovated castle, not all of a sudden out of nowhere as she and Coren walked down a perfectly ordinary hallway in the middle of a perfectly ordinary afternoon. But—*ooch! eech!*—it certainly did feel like ants, or worse. Now that her face was covered they were attacking her hands and arms.

"Coren!" she screamed. "What's happening? What is it? Ow ow ow! Go away, whatever you are! It hurts."

It did hurt, Coren realized. Badly. As he heard Lenora cry out, Coren understood why he was suddenly in such agony— an agony so great he couldn't even speak, not even enough to say "Ow." His face, his arms, his legs—every part of him seemed to be under some kind of very painful attack.

Lenora was obviously feeling it, too—except nothing ever hurt Lenora, and if it did, she'd never admit it. She was certainly admitting it now, and very loudly, too. It had to be something horrible. Yet another disaster, obviously. Coren tried to open his eyes to see what was happening.

He couldn't get them open. Something was pushing against them with too much force. His entire body hurt. And he couldn't catch his breath.

"Coren!" he heard Lenora shout. "The castle—it's gone! Where are we? Open your eyes, for heaven's sake."

Lenora still had the strength to speak, it seemed—even to order Coren around. Surprise, surprise.

Well, it had been at least three weeks since anything really and truly horrible had happened—the longest time he'd made it without experiencing great danger and greater humiliation since he'd first met Lenora not so many months ago. Since then he'd been imprisoned, attacked, embarrassed, insulted, nearly drowned, and had even, for a time, completely disappeared out of existence.

And the result of it all was that he'd fallen deeply in love with Lenora and could not imagine life without her. If the truth be known, in fact, he'd been getting a little bored with how peaceful things had been lately—not that he'd ever admit that to Lenora.

Well, this was an obvious reminder that being bored wasn't so bad after all. Ouch. He tried desperately to open his eyes. Finally, after much effort, he succeeded, only to discover he was staring at nothing. Nothing but white—an empty white that nevertheless felt like a blanket of thorns enveloping him.

Quickly closing his eyes against the onslaught, Coren tried to get his bearings. What had happened? Just now he and Lenora had been in the hallway, on their way from the exhibit hall in the central part of the castle. And now this.

Coren tried once more to pull his eyes open. No hallway.

No castle. Nothing but painful white. He shivered in fear.

Lenora was shivering, too, but not from fear. She was freezing cold. The wind howled and the white stuff that surrounded her remorselessly stung her face and bare arms and legs.

Oh! The white stuff! Of course! She knew what it was!

A while ago, when she'd traveled out into the Gepethian countryside and the weather had gone all haywire, she'd been caught in something called snow. This was it! It was snowing!

She grabbed Coren's arm. "It's snow, Coren. Snow."

Coren had never felt snow before. He didn't really know what she meant, or how it had managed to disappear his home altogether and make his body shake so violently. And whatever it was, he couldn't speak because his lungs seemed to be paralyzed.

Remembering what had happened the last time she'd encountered snow, Lenora knew that she had to act or they would both freeze to death. Still hanging on to Coren, she looked for help.

They seemed to be surrounded by the white stuff, but now that she had got over the shock and was able to gaze into it a bit more steadily, she could see that it was not simply empty white. There were people in it, people so bundled up and covered up that they hardly even looked human anymore. They slogged through the deep drifts that covered the ground, with their bodies bent forward and faces turned downward to ward off the biting wind, completely oblivious of her and Coren standing there just a few feet away from them. Meanwhile, vehicles of various sizes rolled by on what appeared to be a road beside them, their sounds muffled by the roaring wind.

The wind howled so loudly that when Lenora tried to shout at some of the passersby to get their attention, they didn't seem to hear her. They just kept trudging right on by, heads down, to wherever they were going.

Well, then, they had to be going somewhere. Yes, there were buildings nearby—buildings looming like gray fortresses through the thick snow and raging wind. If she squeezed her eyelids together, she could make out a building not ten feet away from her, just past the row of people.

They'd have to get inside, and soon—Coren's face, she could see, was turning distinctly blue behind the now purplish freckles that dotted its surface. And he was definitely not going to be able to open his eyes because the snow had settled on his long red eyelashes and, it seemed, turned to ice. His eyes appeared to be permanently shut.

If they moved toward the building, they could follow along the wall until they came to a door. There had to be a door. She grabbed Coren's hand and stepped forward, pulling him after her.

Almost immediately, one of the bundled-up people walked right into her and nearly toppled her to the snow-covered ground.

"Hey!" a male voice snapped from within a fuzzy red mask that covered his face. "Watch where you're going!"

Lenora fumed. The person in the mask hadn't even looked to see if there was someone or something in his path—and then he had the nerve to tell *her* to watch out!

She couldn't afford to chase after him, though—not in these awful circumstances. Now that she was closer to the building, she could tell that there was nothing but windows, filled with bright colors and objects, all along the wall as far as she could see. There didn't seem to be any doorway or any way in at all. Meanwhile, Coren's thin hand in hers felt as if it were made of ice, and it shook so much that her own hand and arm were going up and down uncontrollably also. Or maybe that was just her shivering, too. They needed help. They needed to find a warm place, and fast.

Lenora could see another person approaching. A woman, maybe—it was hard to tell under all those clothes. Lenora placed herself firmly in the woman's path.

"Please, ma'am," she shouted into the wind as the woman got near. "We need help. We seem to be lost, and—"

The woman looked up. "I don't know what kind of stunt you're pulling," she screamed over the wind, "but you'd better get inside, fast!" And she waddled off.

Frustrated, Lenora pulled Coren forward, narrowly avoiding a few more bundled bodies, sticking close to the wall of windows in hopes of finding a door. Finally she saw a crowd of people turning toward the wall of the building and then disappearing into it. There must be a door there! Dragging Coren, who seemed to have frozen into an unmoving lump, she managed to make it over to the crowd, which quickly surrounded them and pushed them ahead. Before she even knew it, she and Coren were inside. And it was warm, beautifully warm!

Just in time, too. She was shivering from head to foot, and her hands and feet felt numb. She pulled Coren away from the door into the warmer air.

For a moment he just stood there shivering. Then he put his fingers on his eyelids and began to scrape away the ice that held them together. Finally he opened his eyes and blinked. He stared at Lenora, took a deep gulp of air, and gazed around in total bewilderment.

"Wh-wh-what was that? What happened? And where are we?"

## Chapter 2

Coren looked around. They seemed to be in some sort of large indoor courtyard, all done in astonishingly ugly shades of pink and turquoise—Lenora's flighty double, Leni, would probably have loved them. There was polished pink marble under their feet and an expanse of glass set into turquoise frames high over their heads, through which nothing could be seen but more snow.

On a number of tiers of railed balconies around the court-yard, people were walking, most of them dressed in heavy jackets and high boots as if they were still outdoors. Directly ahead of Coren and Lenora, down a few steps, was something that looked a little like a giant version of a child's toy clock tower, also in the same awful pink and turquoise, but with impossibly gaudy gold embellishments and surrounded by lush green vegetation.

On either side of the tower were moving stairways of glisten-ing metal that magically carried yet more people up and down between the levels. The corridors that connected to the court-yard seemed to be lined with open-fronted rooms full of brightly colored objects—toys, games, racks and racks of clothes—and still more people, who were picking up various objects and, it seemed, discussing them with one another and then putting them down again. Large signs with numbers on them were positioned among the objects—the people here seemed to be as obsessed with numbers as the Skwoes out in the Andillan countryside were. Noise filled the air—three or four different orchestras seemed to be playing at the same time, so that no single tune could be heard. And the odor that assaulted them was overpowering, a strange blend of many kinds of food—meat, spices, other things Coren had never experienced before—and a lot of very strong, sweet smells, many of which seemed to be emanating from one of the open-fronted rooms over to the right (the sign over it said ORGANIC PARFUMERIE) and which were threatening to make Coren sneeze.

It was a palace, maybe—the royal seat of some deranged monarch with excruciatingly bad taste and lots of time to indulge it. Or perhaps it was an indoor marketplace—that would account for the food smells, at least, and the racks of clothes that the people all seemed to be arguing about. Or maybe it was some strange blend of the two.

Whatever it was, there was only one possible explanation for it—and for them suddenly finding themselves in it. Coren turned his gaze toward Lenora.

"All right," he said in a resigned voice. "What got into your head this time, Lenora? What have you been imagining, and why?"

Rubbing her hands together to warm them up, Lenora glared at him.

"Don't look at me!" she said angrily. "I didn't do it. Honestly,

Coren!" But, Lenora thought, she could hardly blame him for hoping it was her, even if it was extraordinarily insulting of him to do so. This awful place was definitely not her style, and Coren ought to have realized that right away. Pink and turquoise together in one place, when they were bad enough each on their own.

But if it wasn't her, then who knew what awful force or being had them in its control? Surely their enemy, Hevak, couldn't be on the loose again? Well, there was no point in just standing around and being frightened. Time to do something about it.

"Let's see if we can figure it out," she said. "The last thing I remember, we were there in the hallway, discussing that new Frandilgian exhibit where there are five-day weekends and where everyone blends into one single being and there are no wars or fights or even mild disagreements, because nobody is really separate from the one being anymore. I still think it's a horrible idea, I don't care what you say. And I was just about to tell you that when—when suddenly we were out there in that awful snow."

Lenora was talking about the big exhibit back home in the castle. "A Meeting of Minds"—that was its name. As a celebration of his and Lenora's upcoming wedding, their parents had devised a contest, and the exhibit was the result of it. The idea for the contest came from Lenora's distress with what she'd been learning lately about the way things happened in her own country, Gepeth, and also in Coren's country of Andilla, and from her determination to create a better world than her parents seemed to be content with.

She could do it, of course—she and the rest of the people of Gepeth had the ability to bring whatever they imagined into existence just by thinking it real. Her parents and Coren's, afraid of what she might make of reality without any guidance from more mature and more careful minds, hoped that the contest would help control her wilder urges. Guests from all over had been invited to enter their concept of a perfect world; and also, their concept of the worst world imaginable. Models of these worlds would be put on display in the castle in Andilla, where all the wedding guests from across the worlds could view them and discuss them, and a panel of great minds had been chosen to judge the entries and choose the winners. The best suggestions and ideas would then be agreed to by everyone and become law on the day of Lenora and Coren's wedding—and the worst visions would help everyone avoid any pitfalls.

That was the Meeting of Minds exhibit. Every day, new and wonderful creations arrived. Lenora and Coren found themselves spending all their time arguing about which ones were the best. As well as being enormous fun, these heated discussions had been helping them avoid all the awful, boring wedding arrangements. They had been in the middle of just such an argument, over the desirability of five-day weekends, when—well, when everything changed.

Lenora looked back to where she could see the white stuff swirling tempestuously against the glass doors. Even the thought of it made her shiver again. Where were they? And why was it so cold? As she shook the now melting snow out of her hair and off her long blue skirt and sleeveless silk blouse, she was grateful that at least she wasn't wearing sandals, as she usually did. She'd put real shoes on this morning because sometimes there were tacks or nails lying around in the exhibit hall—even Queen Savet's trusty broom couldn't keep up with the mess the enthusiastic exhibitors were creating as they unpacked their displays and put them together.

Coren had on pants and low-cut boots and that silly loose cotton shirt he was so proud of—he was slightly warmer than she was, but not by much. And he was still shivering, the poor darling. Although it probably wasn't from the cold anymore—she herself was actually feeling quite comfortable. He was just frightened.

She brushed the wet remains of the snow out of his red hair. "That white stuff is snow, Coren. It melts into plain water, like this, see?" She shook her hand, sending drops of water flying through the air. "We could've frozen to death out there. Thank goodness we managed to get inside here before it was too late."

Looking around the courtyard, Coren wasn't so sure that being inside was all that much better than being outside. The gaudy colors were just the beginning. All the people had grim looks on their faces, as if they were miserably unhappy. They hurried from one place to another, carrying shiny bags or dragging screaming children. The artificial light was harsh and made him feel slightly ill, and for all the awful perfume and food odors, the air smelled stale, as if there hadn't been anything fresh, like a real flower or a breeze, in there for years. He had been in the garbage dump in the Skwoe town, and that had been bad. He had been lost in the gray nothing, and that was worse. But somehow this unsettling place seemed even scarier.

Not to mention that they'd been brought here against their will and without their knowledge.

"Get us home!" he urged. "Fast."

Of course. Lenora had been so caught up in the perplexing events that she had forgotten how simple it would be for her to get them home again. All she had to do was use her powers and imagine them there.

Lenora shut her eyes and imagined herself and Coren back in Andilla, back in the same hallway they'd just been walking down. But when she opened them again, the music still blared and the food smells still surrounded them.

"It's not working," she sighed.

"Not at all?" Coren asked, horrified. "Your powers are completely gone?"

"I'm not sure," Lenora said. "I'll try something simple. I'll try to imagine us in some warm clothes."

She tried. Nothing changed. The water still dripped from her light silk skirt.

Of course it wasn't working. These days, it seemed, her powers hardly ever worked. Ever since she'd first met Coren, they had got into scrape after scrape together (although, to be honest, most of them turned out to be her fault and not his—which was very annoying of him). And each time they got into trouble, her powers seemed to disappear for a time—as did his. By now she was almost expecting it to happen.

Each of the previous times Lenora had lost her powers the cause was different—although, come to think of it, that annoying Hevak was always involved somehow. But now, surely, after recent embarrassing events she would prefer not to remember, Hevak was gone for good. What could account for this now?

Coren obviously thought he knew. "All right, Lenora," he said sternly. "Let's think. Just who have you made mad recently? It's got to be someone, or else why would we be here? It's obviously some sort of horrible place people are sent to when they've been bad, or . . . or maybe some kind of prison or something. That means someone who hates you must have sent us here."

Lenora gazed around, her eyes falling on a child screaming, "I want ice cream! I want ice cream!" as a furious-looking woman pulled him by the arm toward the door. She was afraid that Coren might have a point. No one who liked her would send her here. So she must have another enemy, one more powerful than she was herself.

Lenora sighed again. She was supposed to be the most powerful person around, famous throughout her homeland of Gepeth for the strength of her imagination. And every time she blinked, it seemed, there was somebody *more* powerful pushing her around and taking over her life. It was hardly even worth *having* powers anymore.

A new thought struck her. "Wait a minute," she objected. "Why are you assuming it's me that has the enemy? You're here too, after all. Just who have *you* made mad lately?"

Even as she said it, she realized how unlikely it was. After all, Coren was completely nice all the time. The only person who even mildly disliked him was his double, Cori; and Cori, who lived for knightly feats of strength and heroism, simply dismissed Coren as a cowardly weakling—he was too obtuse to see Coren's inner strength. Coren couldn't possibly have an enemy—could he?

"I . . . I can't think of any enemies." Coren blushed. It was a terrible thing to have to admit—being so extremely insignificant and harmless that nobody would even bother to be very annoyed by him.

"Are *your* powers working?" Lenora asked. Normally Coren and his people could read one another's minds. If he still had his powers, maybe he could focus them on whoever it was that was responsible for all this. They'd find a way out of here even if she couldn't do anything herself.

But Coren shook his head and looked even glummer, if that was possible. "Nothing. I can't even hear *your* thoughts, let alone all these other people's—although, considering how miserable they look, I'm not really sure I *want* to know what they're thinking. It's bound to be depressing."

"That's one bright spot, at least," Lenora snapped. "Never having a thought to yourself can be very irritating."

Coren bristled. "Just as irritating as having someone constantly reshuffling the world around you," he shot back.

For a moment they glared at each other. Then Coren said firmly, "I'm sorry, Lenora. I didn't really mean it, and I know you didn't either. It's foolish of us to turn on each other when we have a real enemy to worry about. Please forgive me."

"Of course I forgive you," Lenora said. "As long as you forgive me." She went over and hugged him and gave him a kiss. There was no question about it—Coren was the nicest, most lovable person in the known worlds. He couldn't possibly have an enemy.

And yet, she thought as she lingered in Coren's embrace, here they were, transported somehow to a strange and upsetting place, with no powers and no idea how they got there and no way to get back home again. It was bound to turn out to be her fault somehow. Life was totally and completely unfair. Except, of course, for the kisses. She gave Coren another one and he gave it back. It made even this awful place seem bearable.

Meanwhile, though, they were in trouble. Deep trouble. And Lenora had *no* idea how to even begin to get them out of it.

## Chapter 3

"We need to find out where we are," Coren suggested. "Then maybe we can figure out how far we are from home and how to get back there."

Lenora glanced around for a friendly looking face. There wasn't one. Everyone seemed to be either very tired or very sad or very angry—sometimes all three at once. She finally selected a girl coming out of one of the open-fronted rooms who looked to be about her own age. "Excuse me," Lenora said.

"Yes?" the girl said.

"I was wondering, miss, if you could you tell me where we are?"

"Because," Coren quickly added, "we're from . . . well, from far away. And we're lost."

"You're in Portage Place, of course," the girl said in a matter-of-fact voice as she continued to chew loudly on some substance in her mouth. She had hair the color of daffodils, an unusual yellow to be sure, and she had a jewel stuck into the side of her nose and another one in her eyebrow. Her face was very pale and her eyes were ringed with thick black marks. Lenora knew what that was—makeup. Her double, Leni, adored makeup. It was one of the many things about Leni Lenora disliked.

"And where is that exactly?" Coren was saying. "Portage Place, I mean. Is it a meeting hall? A palace?"

"Well, like, I dunno. It's downtown. It's certainly not a palace—it's a mall, of course. Man, you guys are *really* out of it. Buy a map!"

"A map," Lenora repeated. "Good idea. What does 'buy' mean?" Did it have something to do with bartering, perhaps, or maybe trading things for points, the way the Skwoes did?

The girl gave here a strange, disgruntled look. "Yeah, sure. Consumerism stinks. Big business is out to get us. Yadda, yadda, yadda. I should've known. Look, I'm not joining any weird cult or anything, so lay off. I'm outta here."

She started to move away. "But," Lenora called after her in desperation, "what is your *world* called?"

"My world?" The girl came to a sudden halt, then turned and looked at them. As she turned, her coat swung open, and Lenora's gaze was immediately drawn to a bright light that came from within it. It was eyes—not real eyes, Lenora quickly realized, just pictures. Under her coat the girl was wearing a black top with an oddly shaped gray face painted on it—a gray face with a thin nose and mouth, and huge, oblong eyes that glowed like fire. Over the top of the face were the words THE TRUTH IS OUT THERE.

"You don't know the name of my *world*?" the girl continued, her eyes now so wide they seemed to match the ones depicted on her shirt. "*Where* did you say you were from?"

"We didn't," Lenora answered matter-of-factly. Because they hadn't.

The girl gulped as if she were frightened. "You're right," she said, "you didn't. Of course you didn't. Well, where *are* you from? You can tell me. Your secret is safe with me, I promise you."

Secret? What secret? "I'm from Gepeth," Lenora said, "and Coren here is from Andilla."

"Gepeth? Andilla? Never heard of them. Which means— they aren't here in Winnipeg, right? Am I right?"

"That's right," Lenora said. "What was the name you just said? Win-a-what?"

The girl swallowed again and looked at them intently. She lowered her voice. "Are you . . . are you from Earth at all? Are you from . . . *out there?*"

"Earth?" It sounded vaguely familiar. Lenora looked at Coren. "Coren, are we from Earth?"

Coren considered for a moment. The girl, staring at them, seemed to sway as if she were dizzy. "From the reading I've done," he said, "I believe that part of the physical place our worlds inhabit has, at some time, been called Earth. So, yes, I'd say so. We're definitely from Earth."

The girl shook her head. "This is too weird! A parallel universe, maybe," she muttered to herself. She paused and gave them a suspicious look. "Are you putting me on?"

"What does that mean?" Coren asked. "We're not even all that near to you."

She examined them closely for a moment or two, then her face turned angry. "You *are* putting me on! You're dressed like those Mindies who spoil the convention for us serious people! You saw my T-shirt and you think I'm crazy to believe in aliens and you thought you'd have your little joke. Ha, ha, real funny. So funny I forgot to laugh."

"But—"

The girl totally ignored Lenora's interruption. "You make fun of me, me of all people! I have my certificate in cosmetology, you know! And meanwhile, you walk around looking like half-baked characters out of some stupid fantasy. Well, let me tell you something," she continued, really furious now, her eyes filled with passion, "what I believe makes sense. It isn't any fantasy. There *are* aliens everywhere around us. We may not see them, but why would we? They're way smarter than us. We won't see them unless they want us to! So don't make fun of me, weirdo geek nuts. I'll have the last laugh!"

Lenora's heart sank. This sick-looking girl had started out being helpful, but it was clear now that she was crazy. She actually seemed to think that they'd be surprised by the idea that different kinds of beings existed. Aliens, she called them.

"What do these *aliens* look like?" Lenora asked.

"Like this, of course," the girl said, pointing to her T-shirt. "Not that you really care. You Mindies are so busy being mindless, you don't realize the difference between your silly fantasies and real science. If you ever came *to* one of the *serious* sessions at the convention, you'd soon find out the truth. It is out there, you know!"

Lenora looked again at the glowing eyes. Well, it was a cute little face, and Lenora could readily believe it existed, somewhere or other. Why not? But this poor girl didn't seem to realize what else was out there. Apparently she had never met a Kirtznoldian tree-person or a Drabniggian threebie or even a Gepethian with a strong imagination, like Lenora herself. Probably never had tea underwater with a tentacled Erflumite or even been invited to the six hundredth birthday party of an invisible Vallion—and as anyone back home could tell you, those parties were about as regular as sunrise, because the Vallions simply lived to entertain others and did it all the time. The girl actually didn't seem to know that any kind of creature existed except those little big-eye things and the kind she was herself. Whatever that was.

But if the girl thought they'd be surprised by the idea of aliens, then maybe everyone else here was just as ignorant as she was. Maybe none of them knew anything at all about the rest of the worlds, just thought they were alone in the universe and that other kinds of beings were imaginary, only fantasies.

What a chilling thought—how lonely they must feel, and no wonder they all seemed so angry all the time. Somehow, for some reason, someone or something was keeping them in ignorance of reality. This place *had* to be some kind of prison or place of punishment, no question about it.

As the girl stood there fuming at her, and Lenora thought about what she had said, Coren's mind turned in another direction. "Excuse me, miss, but what was that you were saying about a convention or something?" he asked. "And about our being dressed up like somebody?"

The girl rolled her eyes. "Yeah, sure, you don't even know what I'm talking about, do you? And, like, Elvis is really dead. I've had enough of you two. Go back to your stupid weirdo fantasy friends and leave me alone." She turned and began to stalk off.

"Incidentally," she added, turning back to give them one last disdainful look, "if you *really* want to learn something, which I doubt, then go to the 'The Truth Is Out There' session at three o'clock. It's all about abductions."

"Abductions," Lenora said, turning to Coren. "Now that's an interesting idea. Do you think maybe that's what's happened to us?"

Coren shook his head. "Lenora, I have no idea what's happened to us. All I know is, whatever it is, I don't like it. I don't like it at all. If that girl thinks we're wearing some kind of costume or—*oof!*"

It was a small child—a girl, maybe. She had hurtled into Coren without even seeming to notice he was there, knocking him off his feet for a moment. And now, before they could ask her if she was all right, she was off again, a look of stark terror etched on her face.

As Coren and Lenora watched her go, two other children ran past and after her, in hot pursuit.

*Two against one,* Coren thought. It was totally unfair, and Coren couldn't stand unfairness of any sort. "Let's go, Lenora," he said as he headed off after the children. "She needs our help!"

*Amazing,* Lenora thought as she rushed to catch up with him. *He's terrified of a little bad weather outside and a few grumpy people and some bad taste in decorating inside, and then he rushes off to help someone in trouble without even a thought. How could anyone help but love him?*

# Chapter 4

Lenora and Coren rushed up to where the two bigger girls had cornered the smaller one, in the foliage just by the base of the clock.

"Give it over," one of the bigger girls was saying in a belligerent voice.

"No," said the small girl almost inaudibly, pasting herself against the clock base. "I won't. You can't make me."

"Oh yes we can," said the bigger girl menacingly. "I want it and I'm going to have it."

"She is," said the other big girl. "She always does, don't you, Minnie?" The other girl nodded. "So why don't you just give it to her and save yourself some trouble?"

"But I just bought it," the small child whined. Lenora could see that she was clinging tightly to a fuzzy little toy bear. "It's mine! Mine!"

"But now *Minnie* wants it," the big girl said.

"So hand it over to me," Minnie added. She latched on to the toy bear and began to tug. The little girl looked terrified, but she tugged back.

Lenora bent over and grabbed the two bigger girls by the backs of their jackets. As soon as she did it, the one trying to steal the bear let go of it and began trying to punch Lenora. The little girl immediately ran down the corridor shrieking, "Mommy! Mommy!" and disappeared from view.

Meanwhile the two other girls kept trying to turn and hit Lenora. "What kind of behavior is that?" she said, avoiding their blows. "Trying to force that poor little girl to hand over what isn't yours!"

"Let me go! Help!" The girls both wriggled wildly and started to scream. "Stranger! Stranger! A stranger is talking to us! Help!"

Within seconds Coren, Lenora, and the girls were surrounded by a sea of angry faces.

"Take your hands off my daughter!" one woman shrieked, grabbing at one of the girls and pulling her away from Lenora. Lenora was so startled that she accidentally let go of the other girl, who sprawled awkwardly on the floor and began to moan. "Owwwww! My foot! Owww!"

"How dare you?" another woman screamed as she scooped up the girl from the floor and held her in her arms. "Big bully! There, there, Minerva. Mommy's here now."

"And in broad daylight, too!" a man said as he watched the woman wipe tears from her daughter's eyes with a piece of soft white paper she had pulled out of a small leather satchel she was carrying. "You just aren't safe anywhere these days!"

"Absolutely nowhere," a woman agreed. "I blame the educational system."

"Oh dear, oh dear, oh dear," the mother said as she dabbed at her daughter's eyes. "I hope Minerva doesn't have nightmares because of this. She's had so many awful nightmares. She's so sensitive, the poor dear, aren't you, Minerva darling?"

"Yes, Mommy," the girl said between sobs. "I'm really, really scared, really, really." Then she got a gleam in her eye. "I wonder if those mauve velour jeans we saw at Le Chat d'Eau would make me feel better."

"But Minerva darling, they're so expensive, much too expensive, and I just bought you—"

"*Wahh*," the girl suddenly sobbed loudly. "She grabbed me, Mommy! She scared me!"

"Me, too!" the other girl howled. "Me, too! I want jeans too!"

The crowd all turned to Coren and Lenora and glared at them.

"Bullies," they murmured. "Monsters!"

"I'll call security," a young man said. He turned and ran down the corridor.

"You deserve to be taken out and hanged," one of the mothers shouted right into Lenora's face. "Sh, sh, sh," she added, running back to her howling daughter, looking frantic as she patted the girl's back. "There, there, dear. Perhaps you're right about the jeans after all. Why don't you and Abbey go down there and try them on, and we'll join you as soon as we're finished with these . . ."—she gave Lenora and Coren a look of deep loathing—"these hooligans."

"But . . . but . . ." Coren sputtered, so astonished at the turn of events he couldn't find the words to explain what had happened. Before he could think of anything, Minerva leaped up and grabbed Abbey's hand and ran off down one of the corridors, giving Lenora and Coren a triumphantly evil smile as she passed by them.

"You don't understand," Lenora exclaimed, exasperated. "There was another little girl here, a really small one, and your daughters were being mean to her. They were trying to take her toy away from her, so of course I just—"

"Minerva would never do something like that," one of the mothers said. "You think you can get out of this by lying?"

"Typical," the other one added. "Teenagers today. Tsk, tsk. So just where is this poor little girl you were so bravely defending, I'd like to know?"

Before Lenora could reply, a man in the crowd yelled, "Here's security! He'll lock them up!"

Security looked strong, and he looked angry. "Let's get out of here!" Coren said. "Now." He grabbed Lenora's hand and, unceremoniously pushing aside some of the people, pulled her through the crowd.

"Coren!" Lenora objected indignantly as they ran down a corridor, some of the crowd and the big man in the uniform in hot pursuit. "I *want* to talk to Security, or whatever they call him. Those little girls were bad."

Coren shook his head as he ran, holding her hand even more tightly. "I know that and you know that, Lenora—but all those people didn't seem to know it. And I have no intention of being locked up."

"I . . . I suppose not. But still . . ."

By now they had come to another courtyard, this one with a fountain in its center that intermittently sent up huge spouts of water. Coren was panting heavily, but at least most of the crowd had given up on chasing after them, and only one or two were left—including, however, Security. He was huffing and puffing not far behind them, looking even bigger and even angrier. Coren pulled Lenora around the fountain.

"Duck!" he said, yanking her to the ground. "Maybe he won't see us."

As Lenora crouched beside him, grumbling and rubbing the

hand he'd been holding so tightly, Coren carefully lifted his head past the edge of the fountain. Through the jets of water he could see Security just on the opposite side, standing with a couple of other men and looking indecisively around the corridor.

Suddenly Security shouted, "Hey! There they are! Up there!" He and the other men began running toward an open flight of stairs not far from the fountain.

Coren turned to see where Security was heading. Up there at the top of the stairway, leaning over a railing and looking down, were a boy and a girl dressed in clothes that looked very much like his and Lenora's. The boy had brown hair, nothing like his own fiery red, and the girl was much taller than Lenora and not half as beautiful. But Security must have thought it was them, because he was leaping up the stairs, shouting all the way, "Stop! Stop in the name of the Mall Police!"

"Now's our chance," Coren said. He grabbed Lenora's hand again, dragged her to her feet, and pulled her back down the corridor they'd just come through.

"Ouch!" Lenora said as they ran madly through the crowd. "My hand! Stop it, Coren! Stop pulling me! And stop running, for heaven's sake! You're attracting everybody's attention."

Coren came to a sudden halt and dropped her hand. She was right. Now that no one was chasing them, the best thing for them to do was to try to blend into the crowd.

He had pulled her all the way back to the courtyard with the clock in it. "We'd better not stay here," Lenora said. "Those awful mothers might still be around." She didn't actually see them, but safe was better than sorry.

"Look," said Coren. "There's a door back there, behind the clock."

Looking to where he was pointing, Lenora could see the snow swirling against the glass of the door.

"I don't care how many people are chasing us," Lenora declared, "we're *not* going out there, and that's that." She was about to turn and go back when she heard a bell ring. A silver door off to the side of the glass door opened, and a small crowd of people stepped into the little room behind it.

"Going up?" one of them asked her.

"Why not?" Lenora said. Up was as good as anywhere else. She pulled Coren into the small room just as the door magically slid shut behind him.

The little room seemed to begin moving then—it felt like it was pushing up on her feet. It tickled her stomach. It was fun! Coren, however, looked rather worried.

The people that filled the little room stood there, not talking to one another or even looking at one another, all staring mindlessly at the closed door. Lenora was about to ask them how far up they were going when the motion stopped and the doors opened again and some of the people stepped out.

Lenora looked out through the doorway, her heart sinking. They were back exactly where they had started. Well, this was clearly getting them nowhere. She pulled Coren forward, out of the little room, hoping that the doorway to the snow wasn't the only alternative.

Wait—they *were* somewhere different. She could still see the clock and the open-fronted rooms and the glass ceiling over it, as before—but now the glass ceiling seemed closer to them. And there was a railing close by, through which she could look down at the courtyard floor some distance below. They were higher up in the building.

"We did go up!" she said. "How wonderful!"

"Wonderful?" Coren said, swaying uncertainly. "I nearly lost my lunch in there. Snow, bullying children, that Security fellow—and now this. I want to go home."

Lenora sighed. "Since we have no idea how to do that, I suggest we make sure no one is still after us."

Moving slowly and carefully looking in all directions, she pulled him forward. No Security in sight. They walked over to the railing and looked down toward the floor below. No mothers. No crowd.

"But let's mingle for a while," Lenora said. "Just to be on the safe side."

Coren nodded, and they began to walk past the open-fronted rooms filled with things.

"I've never seen so many things in one place in my life," Coren said, staring into a room of glass cases full of sparkling jewelry. "And the people seem so angry when they pick them up and look at them. I wonder why they're so angry?"

"It seems to fit, somehow," Lenora said. "I mean, everything seems upside down here. Look at the way they tried to punish us for helping that child."

"True," Coren said glumly. "There has to be some way for us to get home. But I doubt if we'll get help from anyone around here."

"Can *I* help you?"

The voice came from behind them. Startled, Coren and Lenora whirled at the same time to see who it was.

Chapter 5

It was a young man. He smiled and seemed friendly.

"Yes!" Lenora exclaimed. "You certainly can help us! Finally! We need to know where we are."

The young man gestured proudly at the room just behind him. "You are at the entrance of shoe central—Fitness Experts!" He drew them into a space full of shoes—nothing but shoes, thousands and thousands of shoes. "We've got everything here—anything your little hearts could desire. What would you like? A jogging shoe? An aerobics shoe? Kickboxing? Water polo? Line dancing? Cross training? You name it, we got it."

Line training? Arrow what? Lenora had no idea what the young man was talking about. For all she could make out of what he was saying, he may as well have been speaking another language.

Another language—something suddenly hit her. She turned to Coren. "They speak the same language as we do, Coren—

except for all that ridiculous stuff about the shoes, of course."

"Ridiculous?" the young man repeated, looking alarmed.

Lenora ignored him. "Otherwise," she said to Coren, "we can understand them perfectly, correct?" Coren nodded.

"Ridiculous!" the young man repeated again, panting heavily as if he were short of breath. "She said 'ridiculous.'"

"That must be a clue," Lenora continued. "I mean, it is more likely, isn't it, that this *has* been done by someone in our world? Or else we'd be somewhere where we couldn't understand anything."

Before Coren could answer, the young man spoke. "I assure you, miss," he said, his voice genuinely worried now, "our shoes here at Fitness Experts are *not* ridiculous. Each and every pair has been designed by a team of trained podiatrists and sports professionals and has been tested for a minimum of six months on the fields or courts or dance floors, whichever is appropriate. Each has been approved by the Fitness Design Association and a panel of top designers and models. These are *good* shoes, miss. You must believe me. We sell only the best here." He really was upset.

Lenora was about to tell him that they seemed ridiculous to her—they were all so ugly and they all looked the same and they didn't even have heels, for heaven's sake. But Coren interrupted her.

"She didn't really mean it," Coren assured the young man. "I'm sure she's sorry. Aren't you, Lenora?"

For a moment Lenora glared at Coren angrily. But he was right, of course—no point in getting into more trouble, especially over something as minor as some shoes.

"I'm *terribly*, overwhelmingly sorry," Lenora gushed at the boy, and she faked a gigantic smile, too. Coren shuddered.

"Good," the young man said, smiling widely again, totally

unaware that Lenora was not being sincere. "We pride our-selves here on catering to the most discriminating tastes—such as, I am sure, yours." His smile got even wider. "Would you like to sit down and try something on? We've just received a new stock of top-grade no-skid joggers, especially made for these icy days. See these small spikes? They go right into the snow and ice and keep right on gripping so you can jog outside even if it's forty below! They're on special today, too! Do try a pair on. Just sit over here."

"Sit down," Coren hissed, looking anxiously over Lenora's shoulder. "And do what he says. That Security person is look-ing in here."

Lenora glanced over her shoulder. The big man in the uni-form was there all right, peering through a display near the front, his surly face surrounded by rows of shoes. He must have figured out that those other people on the stairway were not the two he was after.

Quickly, Lenora nodded. She and Coren sat down in the chairs the boy was pointing to, and the boy knelt down in front of her. How sweet! She was about to thank him graciously and tell him that even though she was a princess, of course, she really didn't need that kind of royal treatment, when he grabbed her shoe, pulled it off her foot, and jammed the foot into a small metal vise. Her foot began to lunge at the boy's face, almost of its own accord.

"Lenora," Coren hissed. "Don't! Please don't!"

She stopped her foot just in time. Coren was right. Although the vise looked like a torture instrument, it really wasn't very painful.

"Size eight," the young man said. "What would you like to try? The ice-and-snow specials? Perhaps our exclusive imported peddle-binding driving shoes for long car trips? Or I could show you something from our line of bird-watching footgear? They're top quality—made by New Balance."

New Balance? Now that sounded like something she could use. Lenora hated the Balance back home—the ridiculous rules that established what a person was allowed or not allowed to imagine. It was for the purpose of creating a new Balance and changing all the known worlds that they were holding the Meeting of Minds contest.

But first they had to get back to Andilla. Out of this place—wherever it was.

"What would you like?" the young man repeated.

"Most of all," Lenora said, her voice intense, "I'd like to know where I am."

"But I *told* you," the young man said, his smile looking a little strained for an instant. "Fitness Experts. How about this week's Fitness Experts special? Each shoe has a built-in digital heart-rate monitor and scale, so whenever you want to know how you're doing, just look down at your feet and there you are!"

"The thing is," Coren said, "we're from . . . well, we're not from here."

"Ah," the young man said. "I get it. You're from out of town. Well, then, welcome to Winnipeg!"

"Win a pig?" Lenora said. "Is it some kind of contest? What do you do with the pig after you win it?"

"Gosh," the young man said. "Don't you even know the name of the city you're in?"

"Of course," Coren said hurriedly, hoping he'd heard it right. "Win Peg. It's Win Peg, right?"

"Winn*i*peg."

"Win-eye-Peg," Coren said. "Of course."

"You're not saying it right," the young man said, looking bewildered. "Like you've never even heard of it before."

"But—"

"Never heard of Winnipeg! How odd. How did you even get here, not knowing where you are?"

"We're just kidding," Lenora said quickly. "Of *course* we know where we are. We just *love* this Win A Pig place."

"Winni*peg*," the young man corrected. "Who doesn't love Winnipeg? Who wouldn't? Although," he continued, "I have to admit that it's pretty miserable out today. Minus forty, I hear. Nasty. But just right for these runners!"

Lenora shivered. In Gepeth, of course, it was always the same temperature, as the Balance demanded. Everyone always talked about how perfectly lovely the temperature was, but since it was always the same, Lenora didn't really understand what it meant at all. After her experience outside she was beginning to understand. And she suspected that minus anything couldn't possibly be good.

"And of course," the young man continued, "we Winnipeggers really don't mind the cold! Makes us strong! Makes us healthy!"

"Is it *always* this cold?" Lenora asked.

The young man paused, his face perplexed. "I *think* so," he finally said.

What an odd answer. "Have you always lived here?" Lenora continued.

"I—" He looked even more confused. "I *think* I have." His face changed. "I see there are other customers. I'll wait on someone else while you're deciding, if you don't mind. Do consider the ice runners. Thirty percent off, today only!" He dropped Lenora's shoe by her foot and was gone before they could even begin to reply.

Lenora quickly slipped her shoe back on. "What's a customer?" she asked Coren.

"Who knows?" he said. "This does seem to be some sort of

indoor market, though, doesn't it? Perhaps people come here and exchange goods with each other, like the Skwoes do, or like we Andillans used to do back in the old days before imagination took over."

"That seems possible," Lenora agreed. "Is Security still there?"

Coren peeked over his shoulder. "Not that I can see."

"Good. Let's explore. We're bound to find clues if we just keep looking."

Chapter 6

They peeked out into the corridor. Security wasn't there. In order to get some distance from where they had last seen him, they decided to take the moving stairway down to the level below. The stairway turned out to be less interesting than it looked. You just stood there not moving while it did all the work.

Once down, they walked over to a shop filled with small pieces of paper with pictures and writing on them. They looked a little like books—and Lenora loved books. If these *were* books, they were very short ones. But perhaps these people had short attention spans—who knew what damage that cold outside might do to their brains?

She picked up one of the pieces of paper.

*In your time of sorrow*
*Know that our thoughts are with you.*

What was it? A poem that didn't rhyme? And what was its purpose? Something to do with telling someone how you felt about them, it seemed. In a sad time. But surely even these peculiar people couldn't be so impolite to others they cared about that they would hand them papers like this instead of actually telling them how they felt in person?

She picked up another one. It had a picture of a smiling man on it with a huge stone sculpture of the number fifty just about to fall on his head and crush him. Inside, it said:

*One, Two, Three, Four, Five.*
*You're lucky you are still alive!*
*Happy Birthday.*

She showed it to Coren. "That's mean, isn't it?"

Coren agreed. "I certainly wouldn't like someone to hand that nasty thing to me. What would you say if someone did? Or would you just hand them another piece of paper back, with something even nastier on it? You know, Lenora, I'm becoming more and more convinced that this Winnipeg is a place for people who have taken leave of their senses."

Lenora nodded. "A sort of madhouse, you mean. They used to have them in Gepeth, back in the old days before we could just imagine people like that back to normal again."

"Yes. In Andilla we all enter the person's mind and offer soothing thoughts to calm and heal them. But we used to have those places for madpeople, too, back before the Great Agreement."

"Perhaps that's what it is, then. But what would be the point of putting people like that all together in the same place? It would surely make their problems worse."

"Yes—and that would account for the way they're behaving toward us!"

"It certainly would," Lenora agreed.

"But"—a new thought struck Coren—"maybe the people who put these madpeople together think they *deserve* to make one another worse. Maybe they're being punished this way?"

"Or maybe," Lenora said, "they're just all the figments of *one* madperson's imagination. Maybe we've ended up in someone's deranged creation!"

"Yes!" Coren agreed. "Of course! Just like when we went to Hevak's—" He stopped in midsentence and gave her a look of consternation.

Lenora knew exactly what he was thinking about—their adventure in Grag, Hevak's country. It had all turned out to be *her* fault, a world out of Lenora's own imagination that they had accidentally been sucked into. Surely that couldn't be happening again?

But she'd created that world of Hevak's without even realizing it. There was nothing to prevent her from doing it again.

*It can't be me*, Lenora told herself, *it just can't! Please don't let it be me again, please, please.*

And surely, even in her most imaginative mood, even at her most angry and vengeful, she couldn't have dreamed up a place where people expressed their cruelest thoughts to one another on deceptively jolly-looking little pieces of paper. With a shudder of revulsion she dropped the one she was holding, which seemed to be suggesting that the person it was addressed to ought to lose some weight before he or she crashed through the floor, or couldn't fit through a door.

"Let's get out of here," she said. "Right now."

As they stepped back into the corridor the loud noises and the powerful food odors assailed them yet once more. But this time the odors didn't seem quite so repulsive. In fact, Coren told himself, they smelled pretty good. Very good, actually. Well, he and Lenora had been here for some time now. And they had not eaten since the breakfast of hot rolls and freshly squeezed orange juice Lenora had conjured up for them very early that morning. He was getting hungry.

It seemed Lenora was, too. "Somewhere in all that," she said as she sniffed the air, "is fried chicken." Fried chicken was Lenora's favorite. "Let's go and see."

Following their noses, they soon found themselves in another large, open courtyard. This one was filled with tables, where more unhappy-looking people hunched over and ate from brightly colored trays of food at an incredibly rapid pace, as if the food would be snatched from them at any minute. Around the courtyard there were open counters, behind which smiling people stood and dished out the food.

"Those ones behind the counter look friendly for a change," Lenora said. "Let's go ask them for some food." Sniffing the air again, she followed her nose to one of the counters.

*Straight into more trouble*, Coren thought, following on behind her. On the other hand, maybe she was right—just standing here smelling the food without actually having any was torture. His mouth was watering.

"What'll it be?" a young girl in a strange military-like hat asked as they approached a counter under a sign that said MAJOR SIZZLE.

"Chicken," said Lenora. "Fried chicken, please."

"Of course," the girl said patiently. "Everything we have here at the Major's is fried chicken. The question is, what *kind* of fried chicken?

"Huh?"

"Do you want the Major's Major Combo? The Sergeant Major Minimeal with a promotion to king-size? Do you want the Crispy Major or the Double-Crunchy Major or the Traditional Down-Home Major Goodness? Straight-at-Attention Soldier Fries? At-Ease Curly Fries? Fiery Fries with

El Pollo Majore and Special Regimental Sauce? What'll it be?"

This was even worse than all those shoes. "What do you think we should have?" Lenora asked. "What would *you* have?"

"Oh, well," the girl said dismissively, "I'm a vegetarian, so I'd never eat any of this awful stuff—no offense, miss, but it's bad for the ecology. I bring a sandwich from home. Sprouts on whole wheat. But if I had to eat here, well, I guess I'd go for the Major's Brave Bugle Boy. It's a nonchicken chicken burger with Simulated Fresh-Breath Onion Rings and Flame-Baked Fries. Tastes pretty good—and it's low fat, too!"

Lenora looked at Coren. Low fat? What was that? Whatever it was, it sounded quite awful. "Actually," Lenora said, "I think I'd like something high fat." She turned to Coren. "If they have low fat," she told him, "they must have the opposite."

"High fat, eh?" The girl shook her head a little but then smiled broadly again. "Well, then, how about a Major Munchie. It's a triple-cheese-and-bacon breast-o'-chicken on a king-size kaiser with a Double-Giant Parade Fries and Super Field Marshal Creamo-Shake. That's about as high fat as you can get."

"All right," Lenora agreed.

The girl turned to Coren. "And you, sir?"

"I'll . . . I'll just have the same," Coren said.

The two waited while the nice girl got their food.

"What did we ask for, Lenora?" Coren whispered to her as they waited.

"I have no idea," she said. "I just hope it's some kind of fried chicken."

"That'll be twelve dollars," the girl said after she had finished piling a huge amount of food onto a tray, "and ninety-seven cents."

"What's a dollar?" asked Lenora. "What's a cents?"

The girl smiled. "Very funny. Twelve dollars and ninety-seven cents, please."

"But we don't have any dollars," Lenora objected. "Or any cents."

"That's for sure," the girl said. "No sense at all. If you won't pay, then I can't give you this food." She began to pull the tray away.

Lenora grabbed at it. "But I'm hungry!"

The girl was no longer friendly. Her face turned grim, and she, too, grabbed the tray and tried to pull it away from Lenora. "I'm getting the manager. Gino!"

"Lenora," Coren said, "I don't think we should get into a fight again. We obviously don't have what she wants in exchange for this food."

"But I'm hungry," Lenora repeated stubbornly, tugging on the tray.

A man with a large black moustache and shiny black hair appeared from the back. "What's going on here? Do I need to call security?"

"Oh, no," Coren sighed. "Not Security again."

Although, actually, he hoped Lenora would win this particular battle—the high-fat meal smelled *very* good.

"We're sorry," he said hurriedly. "We're not from here and we don't have dollars."

"Well, what kind of money do you have?" the manager asked.

"Well, you see, we don't have money. We're not sure what it *is*, exactly. Some kind of points?"

The man shook his head impatiently. "All right, kids," he said, "that's enough. Put the food down and leave, or else."

"Excuse me," a voice said from behind Lenora. "I'll pay for it."

Lenora and Coren turned in surprise. Standing behind them were a girl and boy around their age. They had on heavy coats and hats, just like everybody else here. They were even wearing silly-looking brightly colored shoes like the ones in that store. But under her open coat the girl had on a blue shift exactly like one Lenora owned and often wore. And under his open coat the boy had on a loose white shirt and breeches just like those Coren used to wear all the time. They must be from back home, too! And maybe they knew something about how to get back there!

"You two in for the convention?" the girl asked, smiling at Lenora as she reached into a small leather pouch she was carrying and pulled out a small bundle of colored paper.

"If we are," Lenora said shrewdly, "can we eat this food?" Getting home was her main concern, of course—but there was no point in going back on an empty stomach when it might be possible to arrange for a full one first.

The girl laughed. "You're good," she said. Lenora took that as a yes.

"Then, yes," Lenora answered, "we are. In for the whatever you said. Can we eat now?"

The girl laughed even more loudly and the boy joined in.

"Sure," she said. "Go right ahead, Princess Lenora."

"You, too, Prince Coren," the boy added.

These two knew their names! They really were from home! Things were definitely looking up!

# Chapter 7

"**Y**ou two must really be into it," the girl said, still giggling a little. "Pretending not to know about money, even! Cool!" As she spoke she passed some of the colored paper over to the girl behind the counter, who gave her back some shiny metal discs and allowed the four of them to pick up the trays of food. "You can pay me back later."

"Into it?" Lenora repeated as they sat down together at one of the tables. She grabbed the huge sandwich from the tray in front of her in both hands and tried to wrap her mouth around it. It tasted like salt, mostly—salt and cardboard. Wasn't it supposed to be some kind of fried chicken? Oh well, it was filling, at least—and Lenora was very hungry. She took another bite.

"Yeah," the girl said. "Into it. I mean, if I didn't *know* better, I'd think you two really thought you *were* Lenora and Coren."

Her mouth full of salty cardboard, Lenora looked at Coren. What did the girl mean by suggesting they weren't themselves, when she obviously knew they were? And how did these two know their names in the first place?

The look Coren gave her back was just as confused as her own.

"Of course we're really ourselves," Lenora said after a hasty swallow. "But what I want to know is, how did *you* know that? Are you from Gepeth or Andilla, too? Have we met before?"

The girl smiled. "No, we haven't. I'm sorry, I was so blown away by your performance that I forgot to introduce myself. I'm Barb and this is my friend Thomas."

Coren smiled at Barb and then extended his hand, and Thomas enthusiastically shook it. Thomas was tall—about a foot taller than Coren—and lanky. His hair was red, but an unnatural red, and it looked like he'd painted large, bright red, and very artificial-looking freckles all over his face. *Why,* Coren wondered, *would anybody want to do that?* His own real freckles were horrible enough. Barb was short with long hair, blond but an odd color of blond. Like straw, perhaps. It seemed to have the texture of straw. And of course she was nowhere near as attractive as Lenora—not that Coren was prejudiced or anything, of course. The clothes they wore under their coats were, Coren could see, crudely stitched together and made of cheap, thin materials—they'd make any half-decent seamstress back in Gepeth shudder in horror. But for all the impossibly wide seams, they looked so much like Lenora's and Coren's own clothes that Coren had to wonder even more about what could be going on.

"Hello, Barb," Lenora was saying between chews. "And Thomas."

"And you are . . . ?" Barb asked.

"Lenora, of course. Princess Lenora of Gepeth. And this is my fiancé, Prince Coren of Andilla. But you seem to know that already."

"You *are* good," Barb said between small nibbles on a greasy piece of fried potato. "The best I've seen—your hair almost looks real, *Lenora*. Or should I say, 'Your Highness'?" She giggled again.

Thomas giggled also.

"But," Barb continued, "there's lots of competition, *Your Majesties*. You know, I've hardly seen one single Klingon all day. Everyone is Lenora and Coren this year."

"Everyone," Thomas agreed.

Everyone was them? Coren remembered the couple standing on the stairway—the ones Security thought was them and went chasing after. And now there were these two—and others, too, it seemed. *Everyone* was them, they said.

Coren found himself thinking about Leni and Cori. Those two looked like him and Lenora also. They were, in fact, almost exact duplicates of them. Lenora had created them— mistakenly, she would now admit, for the two of them had created more trouble for Coren and Lenora than just about anybody else. Why, that muscle-brained ignoramus Cori, whom Lenora had imagined being like Coren himself but brave and thoughtless, had almost got them all stomped by a giant once—and he'd even taken over Coren's very own private room and filled it with disgusting parts of the various dragons he was always slaying.

As for Leni, well, all she thought about was clothes and the way she looked and, these days, how jealous she was of Lenora for having a huge wedding to plan. Leni and Cori were to marry soon also, but theirs would be a small ceremony, not the ridiculous public spectacle that Coren and Lenora, as important royal personages, had to go through. Leni wasn't even going to have pew ribbons to worry about, and while she did her best to hide it, like the Goody Two-shoes she was, it made her livid.

Could it be possible that Lenora, or someone else, had imagined yet more duplicates? Coren shuddered—one each of Leni and Cori was more than enough.

But if Thomas and Barb and those two on the stairway were meant to be duplicates, they certainly weren't very good ones. They didn't look at all like Lenora and Coren. If they were supposed to be duplicates, then the person who conjured them up certainly didn't have much in the way of imaginative powers.

"Since you're being so cute about it," Barb sighed, "I guess we'll just have to keep on calling you Coren and Lenora."

"Good," Lenora mumbled, her mouth once more full of food. She was actually beginning to like the cardboard taste—if you sort of tried not to think about it too much, it did remind her just a little of fried chicken. "Please do."

"It's kind of fun, actually," Barb continued. "Almost like talking to the real thing."

Thomas nodded. He hardly ever seemed to say anything.

"Although," Barb said, giving Lenora a careful look, "your costumes aren't quite right. Don't get me wrong—they're pretty good, maybe even the best I've seen today. You must have spent a fortune on them. But Lenora would never wear a long skirt like that, and I don't remember Coren ever dressing in a silly puffed-out shirt—he wouldn't have the style to bring it off, poor dear."

Coren felt his face turning red again—what was wrong with his shirt? It was a perfectly lovely shirt—Lenora had told him so, a number of times.

"Well, of course," he said through clenched teeth, "I suppose we should know what we'd wear. These *aren't* costumes. They're just our clothes."

Barb slapped Thomas on the back. "These two are great!

They never break character, even for an instant. It's amazing how convincing it is—especially when you don't look anything like them."

"We don't?" Coren said.

"Of course not. I mean, it's true that Coren is thin and all, but . . . well, there's thin and then there's downright skinny, right? Not that there's anything wrong with being skinny, of course. Right, Thomas?"

"Right."

"And as for Lenora," Barb continued, looking a little embarrassed, "to tell the truth, the way she's described, I always thought she looked more like me. That's one of the reasons I like her so much. She doesn't look anything like you at all—and yet it doesn't even seem to bother you. I'd never be able to do it myself—I'd be giggling away in no time."

"Me, too," Thomas giggled.

"I mean," Barb continued, "how long were you going to keep it up, back there at the Major's? You were getting pretty close to being tossed right outside—or maybe even getting arrested. That's actually why we decided to cough up the cash, right, Tommy?"

"Right," Thomas said.

"You can pay us back whenever," Barb continued. "But not paying for food, attracting attention like that—it confirms what all these outsiders think about us fans already. And that would be bad for all of us. I mean, we don't want to get a reputation as nuts or kooks. Not," she quickly added, "that I'm trying to tell you what to do. I'd never do that. Everyone is entitled to their opinion, right? It's just something to think about, like."

"I am beginning to understand," Lenora said imperiously as she gulped down the last of her cardboard sandwich. "You two are pretending to be us."

Coren rolled his eyes. What was about to happen was obvious. Lenora would barrel ahead with these two and end up alienating them and they'd get nowhere, and there was nothing he could do about it. He may as well just sit back and eat his food. He took a big bite. Greasy, very greasy. But filling. He took another bite.

"No-o-o," Barb said slowly—and a little angrily, "we're pretending to be Coren and Lenora."

"Why?" Lenora asked.

"Why? Why not? Right, Tommy?"

"Right," said Thomas.

"I mean, if you ask me, Lenora and Coren are absolutely the most interesting characters to come along in some time. I love them both."

Lenora found herself feeling a little less upset with Barb than she had been. "You do?"

"Yes. They're so completely wacky! The way they're always getting so totally mad at each other over absolutely nothing! The way they're always getting each other into terrible messes! And Lenora is so pushy and self-centered! And Coren is such a wimp! They're so completely *silly* all the time—that's what makes them so lovable!"

Coren could see Lenora bristling. He would have been bristling himself—if what this girl was saying wasn't so weirdly true. How did she know all that?

"And the best thing is," Barb continued, "the costumes are so easy. No fake noses and tentacles and all that. It doesn't cost you a million bucks every time you want to go to a convention. And the authors are local, you know, so we get to meet them."

Authors? What authors? Lenora suddenly found herself paying more attention.

"In fact," Barb added, "we're just going over for a signing now. Want to come?"

"Yes," declared Lenora, not waiting for Coren to reply. She didn't know what a signing was, or what authors had to do with it, but any lead was better than nothing. And this Barb may have got her relationship with Coren all wrong, not to mention her entire personality—imagine, calling her pushy, of all things. But nevertheless, Barb did seem to know a lot about them—way too much. It made Lenora feel very uncomfortable, as if someone were spying on her or something. She was not letting Barb out of her sight until she figured it out.

"Where are your jackets?" Barb asked as they got to their feet. "You can't go out like that."

"We don't have jackets," Lenora said. "We didn't intend to be brought here, and—"

"That's carrying things a bit far," Barb interrupted. "I mean, we have to go outside to get to the convention center. On a day like today you could freeze to death out there."

"I know," Lenora agreed, shivering at the memory.

Barb and Thomas looked at each other. "Did you walk here from the convention like that?" Thomas asked in an astonished voice, speaking a whole sentence for the first time.

"No," Coren replied. "As Lenora said, we sort of found ourselves here. We really haven't been at this convention yet."

"Oh," said Barb, relieved. "So you parked underground, in the heated garage. Are your jackets down there?"

Lenora and Coren shook their heads.

"Perhaps," Lenora said, "we could just go into one of the little rooms and get ourselves some jackets."

"Little rooms?" Barb said. "Oh, you mean stores. But," she added suspiciously, "you didn't have any money."

Money. It was, Lenora now understood, what you needed to

exchange for the goods in the rooms. "That's right," she said. "Money. I forgot. But *you* have some of this money, don't you?"

"Now, hold on a minute," Barb said. "A meal is one thing— no way I have enough for a couple of winter coats. And even if I did, I'm not about to lend it to a pair of complete strangers." She gave the two of them a strange, perplexed look, as if she were wondering if inviting them along were such a good idea.

"No, no," Coren said quickly. "Of course you aren't. You're carrying the game too far, Lenora. Let it rest for a minute."

"What?" Lenora said.

"I told you," he continued, "that we should have brought our coats. But oh, no, you wouldn't listen. You had to insist we leave the coats behind just because the real Lenora and Coren wouldn't wear them."

It was enough to ease Barb's doubts. "You two are even more into your roles than I thought," she said. "You're just amazing."

Even so, she and Thomas were stumped over the coat question. "You know," Barb said finally, "I think that if we go through The Gulf, there are connecting walkways that might get us there. It's a long way around, but I think we can probably get there without actually going outside."

"That sounds like a good plan," Lenora said decisively. "Let's go."

And she headed off from the table, not waiting for the other three or even stopping to remember that she had absolutely no idea where she was going.

# Chapter 8

"Lenora," Coren shouted, rushing after her as quickly as he could. "Wait up!"

"No," Lenora snapped, "*you* keep up. This is a good lead. Let's not waste any time."

"Well, at least we could try to find out the direction we're supposed to be going before we start heading off any which way. For all you know, you could be getting farther away from this convention center rather than closer to it. And what if you lost the three of us altogether? What if you lost *me*, Lenora?"

Barb laughed as she came up to them. "You two are so totally perfect! Lenora rushing thoughtlessly into things, Coren scared out if his wits over nothing. Thomas, we should take lessons from them."

Thomas nodded.

"I am not thoughtless!" Lenora objected.

"No, of *course* you aren't." Barb grinned and added to herself,

"Just totally perfect!" Coren nodded with satisfaction. Even strangers could see how headstrong Lenora was.

And also, unfortunately, what a yellow-bellied, hysterical, no-good coward he was himself. But Barb was wrong about him being worried about nothing. Not this time. Nor, he told himself, was it the idea of losing Lenora and having to face this awful, hellish place on his own that bothered him. What bothered him was the kind of messes Lenora would be sure to create for herself without him around to talk some sense into her.

Lenora's hand firmly gripped in his, he gestured to Barb to lead the way. It turned out to be the exact same direction Lenora had chosen in the first place.

Lenora threw a long glare his way but decided to say nothing—Barb would just make some comment about how "cute" she was. If Barb wasn't careful, Lenora would give her "cute."

They followed Barb and Thomas through a bewildering series of apparently endless corridors. Sometimes the corridors had windows on both sides, through which they could see the snow and cold outside, and vehicles and people moving below them and even right under the corridor, which the vehicles made shake and rumble—it seemed they were on a level above the road. At one point, the corridor opened up into a large brightly lit area filled with yet more clothes and other things—for some reason Barb called it "The Gulf," although there was no water in sight. As they entered The Gulf a woman wearing incredibly high-heeled shoes and a very tight, very short skirt tottered over to them, holding a glistening amber bottle. She tried to spray them with some sort of noxious substance, saying, "Touch of Evil. Enjoy the luxury of a Touch of Evil?" Barb just shrugged her off and continued walking. Coren wondered why anyone would want to be touched by evil. Especially when doing it smelled so awful. It made him want to sneeze.

"Oops," Barb finally said, coming to a halt at a doorway down a flight of stairs. "I was wrong."

"Wrong?" Lenora said.

"Yes. I forgot about this." She gestured at the door. Through the glass Lenora could see a large gray space with a low roof that was filled with nothing but unmoving vehicles—vehicles and chilling wind.

"The walkway starts again on the other side of the Parkade," said Barb. "But we have to cross all that open space to get there."

"It's just wind," said Lenora. "Let's go."

"Here," Thomas said, coming up behind her. "You can have my coat." He had taken the coat off and was putting it around Lenora's shoulders.

"Why, thank you," Lenora said, snuggling into the coat and giving Thomas a wide smile. He blushed even more impressively than Coren usually did, so brightly that even the lurid red spots he'd painted on himself disappeared into the background.

The look Barb gave him was so chilly it could have put out the main fire in the new kitchen back home in Andilla.

"I'm just being a gentleman," he mumbled, looking down at the floor and turning even redder. "It's what the real Coren would do, wouldn't he?"

*Of course he would*, Coren thought bitterly, *if he actually had a coat to do it with*. The mere thought of going out there chilled him to the bone. He hardly had any room left in his mind to be furious with Thomas for his ridiculously noble gesture, or with Lenora for the big smile she'd given Thomas for doing it.

In the end, though, Lenora worked out a plan. "Because," she told Thomas with yet another infuriatingly warm smile, "it's *so* kind of you, but it doesn't make any more sense for you to go out there without a coat than it does for me." So Lenora wrapped the coat around herself and ran out through the vehicles and the wind and snow, accompanied by Barb. Then Barb came back carrying Thomas's coat, gave it to Coren, and took him over to the other side. Finally Barb went to bring the coat back to Thomas while Coren and Lenora waited for them.

As soon as the four were all together again in another win-dowed and wonderfully warm and windless corridor, they started to walk again. After a few short minutes Barb once more came to a halt.

"I'm afraid this is the end of the walkway," she said. "Darn. It isn't far though—just across the street. See, it's that big, ugly gray building just over there."

It really was no distance at all—so close Lenora could actually almost make it out through the whirling snow. It was hardly worth going through the fuss of trading coats all over again—especially when the answer to their problem might be waiting over there. Before Coren could start to lecture her about being sensible, Lenora shouted, "Let's go!" and barreled down a flight of stairs and out into the wind, Coren, Barb, and Thomas right behind her.

"Wait, Lenora," Coren shouted, but there was no way she could hear him—the wind was howling much too loudly. He was so furious with her that he almost didn't feel the cold that suddenly enveloped him as he stepped outside—almost. It really was like entering a swarm of stinging bees. He stood stock still, too cold to know what to do next.

"This way," Barb shrieked, grabbing his hand and pulling him through the blinding white. It seemed like an eternity before she managed to steer him through another door and inside into the warmth, but it was probably only a few seconds.

"Lenora," he said angrily between monumental shivers as he

brushed wet snow off his flimsy shirt, "how could you be so thoughtless, so completely—" He stopped in midsentence— she wasn't paying any attention to him at all.

"They're all pretending to be us," she breathed, gazing with wide eyes into the huge room in front of her. "All of them. I don't believe it."

Coren turned to where she was looking. Everywhere, walking around them in all directions, were hundreds of people dressed in blue shifts or breeches, hair dyed blond or red, or wearing wigs, dressed just like Barb and Thomas—just like Lenora and Coren often did. If he wasn't actually seeing it with his own eyes, he wouldn't have believed it possible.

"Pretending to be you?" said a tall girl in a particularly ugly yellow wig as she passed by. "That's a good one. Hey, Leese," she said to the shorter girl in the equally ugly blond wig walking beside her, "get a load of this. She's making like she really is Lenora and can't figure out why we're all dressing up like her."

"Cool," said the other girl. "I wish *I'd* thought of that. But," she added as she turned to stare at Lenora, "you're going to have to work harder on your costume. That blouse is much too . . . well, too feminine for Lenora. A tomboy like her would never wear a slinky silk thing like that. If you ask me, it's one of her admirable qualities, right, Stace?"

"Right, Leese. And the way she puts up with that wimp Coren and all his endless whining without hardly ever even complaining about it. That's admirable too—although kind of dumb, if you ask me. My theory is, someday she's going to come to her senses and realize what an impossible geekoid he is and break off the engagement and go out and find herself a real man."

Coren had had enough. "Now, look here," he said with as

much dignity as he could muster. "You people are being in-credibly rude. My name is Coren, Prince of Andilla. This is Princess Lenora of Gepeth. We really are who we say we are, and what we would *very* much like to know is why everyone here is pretending to be *us*! And," he added, unable to stop himself, "I *am* a real man. Just not an idiot, like Cori."

Leese and Stace looked at him and then at each other. Then they started to laugh. Barb and Thomas joined in.

"First of all," Stace said through giggles, "Coren would *never* talk like that. Lenora is the snooty and bossy one, not Coren. You've got it all wrong. And look at that fancy-schmancy shirt. Coren would never wear a dumb thing like that!"

"Actually," Coren retorted, "I made this shirt myself." And he drew himself up even taller. It was his latest project. Since he'd finished refurbishing his room in the castle, he'd been bored, with nothing to do except listen to those silly wedding plans. So he'd decided to take up sewing. "I think this is an *excellent* shirt," he announced. "Don't you, Lenora?"

"Of course it is," Lenora lied. It *was* a bit silly-looking, but she couldn't bear to hurt his feelings. "Didn't I tell you that already? It very . . . well, very heroic." She turned toward the two girls in wigs. "How dare you tell Coren how he speaks and doesn't speak? Honestly. I mean, look at you," she continued, glaring at them. "Criticizing poor Coren, and you yourself don't look a *bit* like me. Your clothes are all wrong. Not that I ever pay attention to my clothes, but I know that I don't own any like *that*." She gave Stace's outfit a dismissive look.

Stace smiled and turned to Coren. "Your friend here is a much better Lenora than you are a Coren. I mean, her totally annoying, arrogant tone of voice, it's just the way I imagined Lenora speaking when I read the books."

"It is, isn't it?" Barb said.

Thomas nodded.

"Annoying? Arrogant?" Lenora fumed.

"What books?" Coren asked.

"*Of Two Minds*, of course," Leese answered. "What else? Why else are we all here? Sheesh."

"And the sequel, too," Stace added. "*More Minds*. That's a good one. And have you read the newest one, *Out of Their Minds*? I was going to wait for the paperback, but I hear it's a real gas and I just can't resist. I'm getting it today!"

Sequels? Paperbacks? "Wait a minute," Lenora said, her voice becoming *very* loud, and, she hoped, even more annoying. "Are you saying that someone has actually written about Coren and me, in some books—and that's why everyone is imitating us?"

"But, of course," Barb said. "That's where we're going, right? To meet the authors." She turned to Stace and Leese. "They're *really* into their roles, these two. I can't even get them to tell me their real names. Neat, huh?"

Leese and Stace nodded happily.

"Come on, everybody," Barb said, and headed into the sea of Lenoras and Corens. "They're supposed to be down this way."

"We'd better have a look at these authors," Lenora said to Coren as she began to follow. "They must be part of this some-how."

*Authors writing about us*, Coren thought as Barb and Thomas led them through the crowd, saying hello to various fake Lenoras and Corens as they went. He didn't like it. He did not like it at all. Didn't authors have to get someone's permission before they put someone in a book? Because no one had asked for *his* permission. And he wouldn't have given it if someone had—it was an invasion of privacy. His life was his own business and nobody else's.

And who were these authors anyway—and how did they come to find out about him and Lenora? Were the authors from Gepeth or Andilla? Were they spies? How much did they actually know?

A series of pictures began to pass through Coren's mind—pictures of himself on his own, himself with his parents and with Keeper Agneth, himself with Lenora. Each one was more embarrassing than the one preceding it. Surely all those awful things weren't actually written down in books for everybody to read and find out about? Because if they were—

"Yes," he heard one of the pretend Corens say to another as they passed by them, "that time Coren goes into Lenora's thoughts while she's naked in the bathtub is pretty funny. But my favorite is when he ends up in her vision making blueberry pies. That's *so* goofy."

Coren felt himself stiffen. Nobody knew about those pies but Lenora and himself. And as for that terribly embarrassing time in the bathtub . . .

He looked around the room furtively, as if it were filled with dangerous monsters. Did everyone here know everything about him? He was feeling more and more trapped. It was bad enough being surrounded by insane people pretending to be him, not believing who he really was. But realizing that all those people seemed to know way more about his private thoughts and embarrassing moments than anybody ever ought to was worse, much worse. No wonder Lenora got upset when he accidentally happened to enter her mind and she realized he was there. It was too awful.

He grabbed Lenora's hand for comfort. She squeezed his. "Don't worry," she said. "We're going to get to the bottom of this. How dare these authors put us in a book? Believe me, I'm going to give them a piece of my mind."

It was a good idea, Coren told himself. Assuming, of course, that Lenora could actually find a piece of her mind to give them that they didn't already have in their possession.

Chapter 9

They had to stand in a very long line, behind what seemed like several hundred pretend Lenoras and Corens. Barb explained that the authors were signing their books at the table up ahead.

"They're actually writing *in* the books?" Lenora said, shocked. She hated it when people wrote in books and spoiled them for later readers. For her, books were sacred.

"Of course they write in them," Barb said. "It makes the books more valuable. Who knows, maybe someday I'll be able to sell my signed *Minds* books to a collector for a lot of money!"

More of that colored stuff, Lenora told herself. And defacing a book by scribbling in it made it more valuable? This money was more important than books? Things certainly were different here.

"I hear," Thomas added, "that if you beg them, they'll sometimes write their names on your hand or your arm—if there aren't too many people in line. I'm going to beg."

"Why," Coren asked, "would you *want* their names on your hand?"

"Because . . ." Thomas paused. "Because . . . Jeez, I don't know," he finally said, looking a little annoyed. "I just do. If they sign my arm, I won't take a shower for at least a week!"

Coren shook his head. The idiot seemed to think that being signed by these authors would make *him* more valuable.

After a long, boring wait they finally came close enough to the front of the line to see what was happening. Two tired-looking middle-aged people sat at a table, fixed smiles on their faces, pens in their hands. They were both small with dark hair, only hers was very long and his was *very* short. Piles of books surrounded them, and a person stood beside them taking the colored papers called money from those in line in exchange for the books. She had a big square of paper on her shirt with the words SANDRA B., MCROBBIE ALLISON BOOKS written on it. The authors had similar squares. Hers said CAROL M., AUTHOR, his PERRY N., AUTHOR. These people did seem to have a thing about putting their names everywhere.

"Thanks so much," the woman author was saying brightly to a rather pudgy Coren who had his own real freckles. "I'm so glad you liked it." The male author sitting beside her just nodded wearily. The pudgy Coren clutched the book tightly to his chest, smiled happily, and walked off in a contented daze.

It was their turn now. Barb rushed forward and asked the Sandra B. person for *Out of Their Minds*. "I've read the first two," she gushed to the writers. "They were *wonderful*, just wonderful. I wish I could come up with crazy ideas like that! What it must be like to be inside *your* minds, eh? Where do you get your ideas?"

"Actually," said the female author, "the first chapter of the first book—about all the colored dogs? That came to me in a dream."

Lenora found that answer very interesting. A dream? About colorful dogs? She herself had had a dream like that, more than once. And it was in the book? Well, she simply had to see the book.

"But of course," the male author quickly added, "I rewrote the dream—rewrote it entirely, remember, Carol? The dream in the book isn't anything like the one Carol actually had anymore."

"If you say so, Perry," the female author said, winking at Barb. "And this is to . . . ?"

"Just make it out to Barb, please."

"Okay, Barb." She wrote in the book and then handed it to her partner.

"Oh, thank you so very very much," Barb said as he signed it and handed it back to her. She looked at what he had written. "'For all those who are also out of their minds,'" she quoted. "That is *so* cute. Thanks!"

The male author sighed and nodded.

Barb turned to Lenora and Coren. "Your turn now."

Lenora stood for a moment, unsure about what to do. Her temptation was to march up and confront these two despicable spies and ask them who they thought they were, going around sticking their noses into her and Coren's business—and even, it seemed, her dreams—without even asking permission. But if they were like everybody else around here, they'd probably call for Security again. Besides which, she needed to know first what *specific* lies they had told.

"I'd better see a book," she finally said. "The one with the dream in it."

Sandra handed her a paperback book. "It's this one," she said. "*Of Two Minds*. That'll be six dollars, please."

"Oh, no," groaned Lenora, "not dollars again. I don't *have* dollars. Neither does Coren."

"A credit card, perhaps?" said Sandra. "We take Vista or Mister Charge. And there's Interactive, of course, if you have a bank account."

As Sandra spoke Lenora opened the book and quickly flipped through it—she just had to know what was in there.

"Coren!" she suddenly exclaimed. "My name is in here! And here's yours, too! It *is* about us!"

The female author laughed. "Is this a little skit you've developed for Perry and me? How sweet! Isn't it sweet, Perry?" She nudged the male author with her elbow.

"Sweet," he said, sounding totally unconvinced. "Would you like us to sign that?"

Yet another accusation of playacting! It was too much. As Lenora glared down at the male author's annoying, hypocritical smirk she totally forgot her resolution to hold her temper.

"Just who *are* you two, anyway?" she said. "And just *how* do you know about us? And how dare you write it all down in this stupid book? And for that matter, what are we doing here in this horrible place? Because you have to be mixed up in it somehow, you must be, and I'd like to know how, right now!"

Hands on her hips, Lenora leaned down close into the male author's face and looked straight into his eyes—eyes which were now filled with terror.

Coren rushed up to the table and grabbed Lenora's arm, trying to pull her away. "Lenora," he said, "please! Keep calm! We're not going to get anywhere by flying off the handle."

As Lenora turned her fiery gaze on Coren and tried to push his fingers off her arm, he tried to calm down the author, who still looked absolutely petrified. "Please forgive her, sir, it's just that—ow! Stop that, Lenora! Ow!"

"I'll stop it when you let go, and not a moment before. Ow!"

"I'm not going to let go and you can't make—*eee*!"

"Great," said the female author in disgust as she watched Lenora and Coren tugging at each other's arms. "Now we have two nut cases on our hands. I *hate* these conventions, I just hate them." She turned to the other author and patted him on his quivering arm. "Calm down, Perry."

"I am calm," he said in a definitely uncalm voice. "Just get them out of here."

Carol M. sighed and turned to Sandra B. "I suppose you'd better call security."

*Just as I thought*, Lenora told herself as she gave Coren's fingers yet another huge pinch. Well, there was one thing she knew for sure about these deranged people—at least they were consistent. She pinched again. Coren yelped a little but nevertheless refused to let go of her arm. In fact, he was squeezing it even more tightly. She was tempted to give him a swift kick in the ankle. He squeezed again. She gave in to the temptation. "Take that!" she declared.

He kicked back. "Then *you* take that!"

As they continued to attack each other Barb stepped up past them. "No," she told the authors, "please don't call security. They're just *really* into their roles. It's cool, I think."

"It's not cool," said Perry N., watching Lenora and Coren struggle. "Not cool at all. It's going too far, way too far. I nearly had a heart attack there—look, my hand is still shaking so much that I probably won't even be able to write my signature legibly."

"Or maybe," Carol M. said, a glint in her eye, "for a change, you *will* be able to write your signature legibly."

Perry N. gave her a dark look.

"But seriously," Carol M. continued, giving Lenora and Coren an appraising look, "if they're just into their roles—"

"No way," Perry N. interrupted. "They're obviously crazy—

especially the girl. See that look in her eye? She's kicking him like there's no tomorrow. Call security, Sandra."

"I have to admit," Carol M. said as she watched Lenora and Coren, now busily trying to stamp each other's feet in between pinches, "that they *are* pretty convincing. They actually look as if they're ready to kill each other—just the way Lenora and Coren would in a situation like this. It's amazing how good they are—especially considering how little they look like the real Lenora and Coren."

"There!" Lenora said with one final tug that finally pulled Coren's hand off her arm. "That hurt! I'll deal with you later, Coren. And," she added, turning back toward the authors, "as for you two—"

The authors cringed as they looked up into her enraged face.

"Now, Sandra!" said Carol M. "Go now! They *are* crazy!"

"How rude!" Lenora said imperiously, her best princess look on her face. "Talking about us as if we weren't even here, saying we're crazy! We aren't crazy—are we, Coren?"

"Huh?" Coren said. Now that he had given up fighting with her, he had picked up the book Lenora had dropped in the midst of their struggle and had begun to leaf through it. It *was* about him and Lenora, he quickly saw—*everything* about them. Him worrying about his ridiculously hairless face. That awful pool and his stupid fear of it. And that time at the banquet in Gepeth when—

"Lenora," he suddenly said, so caught up in what he'd just read that he was now totally oblivious of the horrible situation surrounding him. "Did you actually think *that?*" Pointing to a passage at the bottom of a page, he stuck the book right in front of Lenora's nose.

"Coren," she said. "I am busy at the moment dealing with these rude people." Almost against her will, her eyes began to make sense of the words in front of her—Lenora couldn't help reading anything in print any more than she could stop being Lenora. "And—oh, no!" She grabbed the book from Coren and read the passage again, this time with her full attention. Then she slowly closed the book and looked at the authors uncomprehendingly.

"You couldn't know that," she said. "You just couldn't! Why, I'd never tell an embarrassing thing like that to anybody. I'd die first. How could you—" Suddenly she stopped, her eyes widening as she realized what she was saying—what she was admitting. "Uh," she continued, "I mean, no, Coren, of course not. I'd *never* think that, never. It's ridiculous. It's lies, all lies!"

"Yes," he said, remembering the part about his hairless face. "Lies! Of course it is!" And now he was glaring down at the authors just as angrily as Lenora was. "Lenora's right. You *are* rude. How dare you make up these ridiculous lies about us?"

"Where's Sandra?" Perry N. shrieked. "Why aren't those security guards here yet?"

"You tell us who you are and what's going on," Lenora said, "or I'll . . . I'll . . . well, you don't want to know."

Carol M. spoke slowly, although her face had gone white with fear. "Now, listen carefully to me. We made this up! It's fiction. These characters are *fictional*. None of it is real. You are not Coren and Lenora, because they are only figments of our imagination."

She seemed to be sincere—absolutely sincere. It dawned on Coren that these authors really believed what they were saying. They honestly believed that they had simply made him and Lenora up, conjured them out of their own imaginations.

And meanwhile, he and Lenora believed—rather, *knew*—they were real. It made no sense—no sense at all.

But one thing was certain. He and Lenora needed to have a

close look at that book. No matter how embarrassing it might turn out to be, they had to study it and find out how similar to their lives it really was.

And also, there was the small matter of getting away from all these increasingly angry people before Security showed up. Perhaps, if he sort of inched over to the table, he could grab one of the books and then—

Lenora was way ahead of him.

"Since you have stolen from our lives to make these ridiculous books," she said haughtily, "I'm sure you won't mind if we take one. In fact, I'll take all of them." She quickly grabbed one book from each pile and then turned and began to walk away, saying, "Come, Coren. Our presence here is no longer desired or required. Come now!"

"Hey!" Carol M. called after her. "You can't do that."

"Security!" Perry N. yelled. "Help! Thieves! Maniacs!"

"Stop those two!" Carol M. called out to the crowd that had gathered around. "They're stealing books!"

"Stop!" Barb pleaded. "Now you really have gone too far!"

"Stop!" people began to yell, looking around to try to figure out who they should be stopping. "Thieves!"

As she entered the milling throng Lenora's regal stroll suddenly became a speedy run, and she disappeared from view, shouting, "Hurry, Coren!"

As hands from the crowd began to reach out to grab him, Coren dashed after her.

# Chapter 10

Coren hurtled through the crowd, unceremoniously shoving people out of his path. Couldn't Lenora have just asked nicely? Maybe they would have let them borrow a book.

*Hardly*, he reminded himself. After that pathetic, childish tantrum Lenora had just had, those authors were about as likely to lend them a book as they were to turn into a pile of nicely folded towels. Why couldn't Lenora be sensible and calm, like he was?

*Like I am usually*, he added to himself, remembering his own part in the episode. Why was Lenora so completely infuriating?

Anyway, it was obviously too late now. Much too late. He made a quick shift to the left, thus narrowly avoiding a painful crash into a particularly muscular and painfully solid-looking Coren. As a result, he stomped on one of the Lenoras' toes, but he kept right on running.

Luckily Barb had been right—most of the crowd were dressed up as Lenora and himself, which meant that it didn't take long for the two of them to lose themselves in the horde of other blondes and redheads. They soon found themselves alone at the back of the crowd, standing just inside the entrance to a quiet corridor and panting heavily as they looked back out to see if they were still being followed.

"Nobody there," Coren whispered. "I think we'll be okay—for a while, at least."

"A while is all we need to look at these books. But first we have to find somewhere where we won't be interrupted." Lenora stepped further into the corridor and looked around her. "Here, maybe." She tried the door closest to her. "Locked," she said.

So were three other doors farther down the corridor. There was just one more door to try—the one at the very end of the corridor. It looked just like the other three, except there was a sign on it with fancy letters carved in wood.

"'The Richard Hartleyson Memorial Meditation Center and Nondenominational Chapel of Repose,'" Coren read. "'Feel Free to Leave the Gathered Throng Behind and Be Alone with the Creator of Your Choice. Donations Welcome But Not Required.'"

"'The creator of your choice'?" Lenora said. "That makes no sense. Surely you can't choose who created you. Not even I could do that. But"—she twisted the knob—"it *is* open. And we do want to be alone and find out about these ridiculous books. Let's go in."

It was just a gray box of a room, without windows and with a very low ceiling from which a row of glaring lights hung. But it seemed to be furnished much like the chapels back home in Gepeth—a few rows of mahogany pews that faced the wall opposite the door. Unlike the chapels back home, the wall at the front was entirely covered with a huge picture of a rather garish orange sunset, the only decoration of any sort. Except for that, the room was empty.

"Here," Lenora said, handing Coren a book as she sat down in the closest pew. "You take that, and I'll look at this one."

OF TWO MINDS the book Coren was holding said. It said it twice, in two different colors, pointing in two different directions. How odd. Under the words a very pretty young girl stared out, arms folded. Above her, and upside down, was a dashing young man.

Surely these two gorgeous people weren't supposed to be him and Lenora? The girl was pretty, all right, but she had none of Lenora's majestic presence. Her eyes were disproportionately large and disproportionately gentle—she looked like someone you wanted to protect and look after, whereas Lenora herself looked like someone who wanted to protect and look after you and wouldn't take no for an answer. As for the young man, well, his hair was more brown than red, and there wasn't a freckle in sight. Not a single one. If Coren actually looked like that, he'd have no worries at all.

Coren opened the book and began to read. "The castle was quite empty," it said. It went on to describe a girl conjuring up a series of dogs of different colors that then turned on her and began to chase her down a stairway. Coren recognized the dogs and also the stairway—they'd appeared in his own nightmares many times in the days before he first met Lenora. So why, then, was it a girl who was dreaming about them in the book?

He read on. The girl turned out to be Lenora. It was Lenora who was dreaming about the dogs.

"Lenora," he said. "This dream here—about the dogs. Did you really dream that?"

"Yes," she said, looking up from her own book and giving him a defiant look. "I did. So what?"

"Nothing," he said. *But,* he added to himself, *that would explain why I had those dreams too—I was somehow managing to hear Lenora's thoughts even before I met her. How strange. And I never even knew it until I read it here in this book.*

The authors seemed to know more about what had really happened to Coren than he knew himself. It was bizarre.

"This is *really* strange," Lenora suddenly said.

"You're not kidding," Coren agreed.

"Listen to this," Lenora continued. "It's about Sayley."

Lenora's young friend Sayley was only ten years old, but she had a will as strong as Lenora, and she also had impressive imaginative powers. As Lenora and Coren had learned on more than one occasion, this made life around Sayley almost as interesting as it always was around Lenora herself.

Lenora read aloud:

*"The door suddenly opened. It was the beautiful Princess Letishia, whom ignorant fools insisted on calling by the silly name Lenora instead of her true name. As soon as Lenora heard that the unfortunately downtrodden Sayley was in trouble through no fault of her own, Lenora had immediately given up her glamorous royal life and had come to rescue Sayley and snatch her away from her heartless parents. In no time at all Lenora and Sayley were at a banquet held in Sayley's honor. The food was scrumptious. It would have been perfect if Prince Coren had not been there. Coren was very skinny and pathetically jealous, and he kept unsuccessfully trying to get Lenora to pay attention to him instead of to her true eternal friend, Sayley. Sayley didn't mind—she, of course, was above mere petty jealousy. But poor Lenora loved being with the wondrous Sayley so much that Coren's interruptions made her totally furious."*

"I certainly don't remember that," Coren said. "You *weren't* furious with me—were you?"

"No, of course not, Coren. Don't be silly. That's what's so strange. It's sort of the way things happened—I did go get Sayley, and we did have some food after, remember? But as for the rest—"

Coren nodded. He couldn't decide which was worse—the authors accurately writing down what happened, or them getting it all distorted and so completely wrong. Somehow, both seemed equally awful.

And he wasn't all *that* skinny, was he?

They went back to their reading.

"Lenora," Coren said after skimming through a number of chapters, "this tells about Grag and our meeting there with Hevak, but none of it is quite right either. Listen to this: 'Grag was a country filled with splendiferous creatures—elves, fairies, even scrumptious trolls.'"

"'Splendiferous'?" Lenora repeated. "And 'scrumptious' again?"

"Yes, again. It's about the fifth 'scrumptious' I've noticed in just a few pages."

"I've seen three or four myself, actually. Those authors really like that word a lot. What bad writers."

"Yes. And listen, here's how Hevak is described: 'Some—people with shallow ideas of beauty—would think he was gorgeous, with that greasy black hair and those overly huge shoulders and that fake smile full of oversized white teeth.'"

"Ridiculous," Lenora said. "Hevak *was* gorgeous. His shoulders were broad and manly. And I loved his teeth."

"If you say so. But the thing is—well, these words sound familiar. I mean, I'm sure I myself might have described Hevak like that to someone."

"Come to think of it—I've heard you do it, more than once. You are *so* wrong about Hevak, Coren. I mean, yes, he was incredibly evil—but he was also very handsome. Very, very handsome. My idea of a regal presence."

Coren gave her a dark look. "Speaking of which," he continued, "how about this? 'Of course Prince Coren hardly looked like a prince at all with his face full of freckles and all that impossibly red hair.'"

Lenora shrugged. "Well, Coren, that is sort of true."

"Hmph," said Coren. "The point is, *you* think it's true. It's exactly the kind of thing I've heard you say again and again. It's almost as if these authors knew your thoughts and were putting them in the book."

"I know what you're thinking, Coren, and you can stop thinking it right now. I did not make up those authors or this place. This is not my fault." Then a new thought struck her. "Anyway, if those authors did know my thoughts like you said, well, then maybe they're actually people from Andilla? After all, you Andillans are the ones who go around rummaging in other people's thoughts without permission. Maybe this is *your* fault."

That wasn't even being logical. "The real question, Lenora, is how do these authors know *anything* about Grag, or Hevak, or us, for that matter? It makes no sense. And my head is starting to hurt."

"Mine, too—but there's got to be a clue here somewhere. Keep reading."

"Yet more 'scrumptious'es," Coren said after a short pause.

Lenora nodded. "And listen to this, Coren. It's about Leni and Cori. 'The two duplicates of Lenora and Coren drove everyone crazy, especially poor, blameless little Sayley. They could never appreciate her brilliant imagination.' Do you see what I see?"

Coren nodded. "For a story about the two of us, there seems to be a lot about Sayley in it."

"There certainly does. And what is Sayley's favorite adjective, Coren? What does she call everything she likes?"

"Scrumptious. Of course."

"Of course. And I did tell her all about our adventures in Grag, so she'd know my thoughts about it."

"I told her about that, too, actually—she asked me to, one day not so long ago. It kind of surprised me, since she usually ignores me. So she'd know my thoughts also."

"But," Lenora said, her voice troubled, "Sayley is such a sweet little girl. A little headstrong, but harmless, really. What could she have to do with us being in this awful mess?"

Lenora would never accept how dangerous Sayley might be— the little girl reminded her too much of herself for her to be able to think any truly harsh thoughts about her. Coren was going to answer and tell Lenora it looked very much like Sayley did indeed have a lot to do with it—far too much—when the door suddenly flew open and a pretend Lenora rushed in.

"Oh, good," she said. "I'm not the only one attending the service!"

"Service?" Lenora said.

"Yes," the pretend Lenora said, marching forward and sitting in the pew in front of them. "I'm so glad the convention organizers remembered to include some spiritual moments in the program, aren't you? We should never forget to offer thanksgiving to the power that brought us here. All hail her."

"Her?" Coren said.

"Her, of course. The Divine Sayley."

Chapter 11

Coren and Lenora looked at each other and gasped. "Sayley!" they said together.

"I knew it," Coren added. "That little brat is almost as irresponsible as you are sometimes, Lenora."

"'Little brat'?" the pretend Lenora said in a shocked voice. "You're calling the Divine Sayley a 'little brat'? That's . . . that's sacrilege!"

"Oh, come now," said Lenora dismissively. "That's a bit extreme, isn't it? Sayley is just a little girl, after all."

"'Just a little girl'?" It was a fake Coren speaking now. He had just come through the door and, apparently, overheard Lenora's last statement. "The beneficent power that guides us? The creator of us all? Yes, of course, she does appear to us mere mortals as a harmless young female child. But everyone knows that's just so we won't be overwhelmed by her true celestial presence. The Divine and All-Powerful Sayley is hardly 'just a little girl.'"

"Amen to that," the pretend Lenora said.

"Amen," added two other Corens and another Lenora who had just entered the room.

"Uh . . . Amen," Coren said, not very convincingly—but, he hoped, convincingly enough to distract attention from Lenora and himself. It seemed that no matter what they said or did in this horrid place, they upset somebody. Why were these people getting so distressed about someone who was, as far as *they* knew, just a character in a book?

Fortunately, Coren's "amen" seemed to work—although the first Lenora, who had informed them about Sayley's divinity, gave him and Lenora a very worried look and shook her head at them before she finally turned around, mumbling something under her breath about Sayley protecting her from infidels.

Meanwhile, yet more Lenoras and Corens were arriving— and also a few other people wearing unbuttoned coats but no blond wigs or painted-on freckles. It was actually a relief, Lenora realized, to see a few people *not* pretending to be her and Coren. They seemed so sensible somehow.

One of these people—a tall, somewhat older man with large pointy ears, dressed in what looked a lot like the kind of flannel pajamas Lenora's mother made her wear when she was young—squeezed into the pew beside her. She gave him a welcoming smile.

"Hi," he said, almost brushing her cheek with one of his ears as he nodded at her. "Great convention, huh?"

"Uh, yes, it is," said Lenora, pulling herself out of ear range. "Great. I see you're *not* pretending to be Coren today." Surely someone not wearing a costume would be rational enough to help her understand things better.

"I can't imagine why anyone would ever want to be a little wimp like that," the man said vehemently. "And the stories are so badly written, if you ask me. I mean, there *are* other adjectives in the language beside 'scrumptious.' But of course"—he gestured at Lenora's dress and hair and Coren's freckles—"I can see you don't agree with me."

"Oh, yes," Lenora said, "I do. Don't we, Coren?"

"Not about the little wimp," Coren said. "About the language."

The man smiled. "Well," he said, "it's good to see that at least some of you Mindies haven't taken total leave of your senses, even if you are wearing those ridiculous costumes. The whole series is much too popular to suit my taste. All these newcomers reading that trashy bilge, it just shows how the educational system has failed us. Now, myself, I prefer the classics. I've been Spock for the last, well, I don't know how many conventions, and I intend to keep on being Spock. These good old ears"—he patted them—"aren't going into retirement until I do."

Lenora took a closer look at the ears. They were, she could see now, not real—there were seams where they joined on to the rest of the man's head. So this was also some kind of costume. A costume consisting of oversized ears and undersized nightwear that showed off way too much of the man's somewhat expansive stomach—and he thought that being herself or Coren was silly!

"I wonder," Coren said to Lenora as he looked around at the people who now filled the chapel, "why, if they worship Sayley, no one ever dresses up like her?"

"Dress up like Sayley?" said the man with the big ears, horrified. "Impersonate the Divine Being? That would be sacrilege! Desecration! What an awful idea!"

"I don't understand," Lenora said. "She's just a character in a book, too, isn't she? Just like Coren and Lenora?"

"Oh," said the man, relieved. "*That* Sayley! For a minute there you had me going."

"You mean—the Sayley in the book is not the Divine Sayley?"

"Of course not. She's only named after the Divine One, of course—just a cheap trick those inept authors used to attract attention, if you ask me. Why would anybody want to impersonate *her*?" Then he gave Lenora a troubled look. "How could you imagine that that annoying little girl could have anything to do with the Divine Sayley?" He shook his head back and forth at them, making his ears flop violently, and then slid himself farther down the pew, as far away from Lenora and Coren as he could get.

As this conversation had been taking place, various Corens and Lenoras had been at work, apparently preparing for some kind of ceremony. A portable pulpit had been brought in and placed at the front, and a vase of very artificial-looking flowers had been placed upon it. Someone had touched a small black protuberance on the wall near the door and made a flat white square descend from the ceiling near the front wall, blocking out much of the garish sunset. Now, suddenly, the lights went dim, and the white square filled with a giant face. A child's face.

Sayley's face? No, Lenora thought, not Sayley's face at all. It did vaguely resemble her young friend, very vaguely. But this child was angelic and gentle-looking, and the impish Sayley was certainly neither of those. Furthermore, the child in the picture glowed—streams of light emanated from her perfect head in all directions, much the way Lenora herself had glowed not so long ago, when the Skwoes invaded the Andillan palace.

Except, Lenora had to admit as she gazed up at the giant

angelic face on the wall, take away the innocent expression, take away the glow, and the Divine Being would be an ordinary little girl. A little girl who looked an awful lot like Lenora's young friend.

"My friends and fellow worshipers," a man said from behind the pulpit, "welcome." Through the dim light Lenora could see that he, too, wore a red wig and had freckles painted on his cheeks. But unlike the other pretend Corens, he was wearing a black suit and a collarless black shirt.

"Welcome," the crowd repeated.

"We are gathered here today," the man continued in a deeply solemn voice, "in the midst of playful celebration, to contemplate the purpose of it all. And"—he paused dramatically—"we all know what that purpose is. Bend now in humble submission and say it together with me."

The crowd bent forward. "The purpose," they chanted together solemnly, "is the divine will. The will is the way. What Sayley wants is what is. Praise Sayley! Praise Sayley daily!"

As they chanted, the image of the little girl on the screen changed. The face grew more angelic, somehow, and the glow grew even stronger.

*Just the way Lenora glowed when she took over everything,* Coren told himself as the face shone brighter and brighter. *I don't like this. I don't like it at all.*

Sayley's ears were burning—she could almost feel the glow radiate from them. Her mother always told her that was because people were talking about her. Well, she hoped that they *were* talking about her. In her opinion, she definitely deserved to be talked about, and the talk ought to be nothing but praise.

She was hurrying to the Meeting of Minds exhibit in the

grand ballroom, where her inventions of the perfect world and the worst possible world were on display. She was very proud of those inventions—she had worked diligently and had made them detailed and intricate, right down to the tiny wrinkles on the people's foreheads and miniature buttons on the blouses they wore. Lenora couldn't have done it any better. And now the prizes for the best ideas in the youth contest were about to be awarded, and the first-prize winners would be allowed to submit their ideas into the adult category.

Sayley had carefully examined all the others in her group, and she felt that she had an excellent chance to win both prizes—both the best world prize and the worst world prize. It was amazing how clichéd and conventional most of the displays were—the perfect worlds were all sunshine and flowers and people mindlessly loving each other, and the worst ones all seemed to involve eternal fires and crudely obvious displays of violence and torture.

Her own inventions were nothing like that, nothing at all. She'd planned both of them around some strange white stuff called snow—for some inexplicable reason it had been falling out of the sky the day she and Lenora first met. She'd only experienced it that once, but it had left a lasting impression, and when she heard about the Meeting of Minds contest, it was the first thing she thought of.

Sayley had had tremendous fun working out how a world of snow might be wonderful, truly scrumptious, and also how it might be horrible—and in a few minutes she would find out whether or not the judges were smart enough to understand how scrumptious her creations were. Because, if you asked her, she deserved nothing but praise for them. The mere thought of how wonderful they were just made her glow with pride. No wonder her ears felt so warm.

Just ahead of her were Coren and Lenora.

"Lenora!" she called out. "Wait up!"

Lenora turned and hardly acknowledged her. That was strange, because Lenora was always so glad to see her. "Lenora," she said as she ran up to her, "have you seen my exhibits?"

"Yes," Lenora said in a dismissive voice. "I have. Typical of you. Totally unlike all the others, outrageous in every way."

As Sayley watched, Coren sort of elbowed Lenora and glared at her.

"Oh," said Lenora, "I forgot. What I mean is, very nice, Sayley dearest. Very . . . imaginative."

The words seemed to stick in her throat. This wasn't at all like Lenora. What was going on?

Well, Sayley didn't have time to worry about it now. She shrugged a little, nodded at Lenora and Coren, and hurried off down the hall. There was an award ceremony to get to, and with any luck her name would soon be on everyone's lips. As, of course, it should be.

## Chapter 12

"Sayley, Sayley, Sayley!" the people in the chapel sang, lips all moving together as one. "Thanks be to Sayley for the joy of jubilation and the scrumptiousness of life."

Scrumptiousness. Again. "I tell you, Lenora," Coren whispered, "it *has* to be our Sayley."

"But Coren," Lenora whispered back, "she is only ten, after all, and—"

"*Shhh,*" the people around them hissed.

"Let's get out of here," Lenora said.

Coren nodded. They hurried to the back of the room, the worshipers giving them angry glances as they passed, and out into the corridor.

"You have to admit, Lenora, that Sayley must have something to do with it. 'The scrumptiousness of life' indeed!"

"I suppose so," said Lenora reluctantly. "But it doesn't make sense. Sayley *likes* me. She even sort of likes you, I think. She'd never send us to such an awful place on purpose."

"But she has a lot of power, right? And as we both know"—he gave Lenora a meaningful look—"sometimes people with a lot of power can't control it. Maybe she doesn't even know we're here. Maybe she imagined it for a brief second and that was enough."

"But why can't I imagine us out of here then?" Lenora asked. "Sayley is strong, yes—but I'm much stronger."

"Perhaps," Coren mused, "it has something to do with how unimaginative people here are. I mean, they wouldn't even consider the idea that you and I might really be ourselves. Not for a minute."

They moved down the corridor until they reached a room with an open door. Inside, a very bald man was speaking to a group of attentive Lenoras and Corens. "And as Professor Reimer, of course, suggests," he intoned, "the conflicting worlds of Andilla and Gepeth most significantly mirror the central unresolvable conflict of the human psyche, so that the marriage of Lenora and Coren can always be about to happen but never actually happen."

"See," Coren said as they stood for a moment in the doorway and listened, "they're so busy thinking we aren't real that they've even made us into some kind of symbolic representation of themselves and their own problems. Of course we'll be married—and soon, too."

"Of course," Lenora nodded a little hesitantly as they moved on. She was thinking that the marriage actually wasn't likely to happen until they got out of this awful place, and that didn't look like it was going to be anytime soon. And come to think of it, Sayley, the poor little dear, had always been rather jealous of Coren and would have liked to delay the marriage forever. . . .

A guffaw from Coren interrupted her thoughts. "Listen to this," he said, standing just outside another doorway.

"It should be obvious to all," said a thick-bespectacled woman to a group gathered inside, "that Lenora deeply feels the lack of her parents' love. The obsessive urge of her mother, Savet, to erase all 'dirty' thoughts, represented by her compulsive obsession with sweeping and towels, is matched only by King Rayden's imperious oedipal jealousy of Lenora's power to wound him."

"Wound him?" Lenora said. "I would never wound my father. I love him, and he loves me. How dare that woman—"

"Lenora," Coren warned her, dragging her down the corridor.

"I'd like to give that . . . that *moron* . . . a piece of my mind!" she said. "I'll show her what a wound is! The nerve!"

"Lenora," Coren said, his voice excited, "Look!"

She raised her eyes to see what had attracted his attention.

It was coats, rows and rows of coats hanging up on racks. Why was Coren getting so excited about a bunch of coats, of all things?

"We can, uh, *borrow* some of these and get out of this place!"

Lenora could see that it was a good idea to get as far away as possible from the various people they had annoyed. But go out into that awful snow?

"Why would we want to go outside?" she asked.

"Well, I was thinking—about the Skwoes. Maybe it's the fact that these people believe we aren't real that's blocking our powers. And this convention thing is a gathering of people who like to read about us. So if we get away from all these people who know about us but think we're just characters in books—"

"It's possible," she agreed. She headed over to the row of coats and began to pull one off its hanger. It wouldn't come off.

Coren examined it. "Why, they've got it locked up. Look!" He pointed to the chain running through the arm of the coat.

"But why would they lock up their coats?" Lenora asked. "That makes no sense at all, especially when its so cold outside."

"Maybe," Coren mused, his eyes filled with suspicion, "maybe they knew we'd want one."

"All this just to stop us from going outside?" Lenora snorted.

"Who knows?" Coren said. "Why else?"

Lenora couldn't think of another reason. Finally she said, "If you're right, we *have* to get some coats and get outside. They must be trying to stop us for a reason. Surely there's got to be one somewhere in all this mess that isn't locked up!"

She pushed her way into one of the narrow pathways between the racks of coats, tugging desperately (and unsuccessfully) at their sleeves as she went, and soon disappeared from view.

Typical, Coren thought, Lenora rushing off thoughtlessly when there was clearly a much better solution to their problem. He had been examining one of the coats, feeling some dismay about the awful workmanship—the seams weren't even double stitched, let alone oversewn, as surely any sensibly made garment would be. Which meant that it would be easy to rip open the seam and free the coat. A coat with an open sleeve would probably still be warm enough—they could just keep the one arm wrapped up inside the coat. It would certainly be better than no coat at all. He was about to call Lenora back when she called him.

"Coren!" she said. "Come here! Take a look at this!"

He pushed his way through the coats. Behind them, where there ought to have been a wall, there wasn't. Not only was there no wall, there was—well, nothing. A huge expanse of nothing. Looking at it was something like looking out from the edge of a high precipice—except there was no valley below, no cliff face on the other side. Just nothing.

Lenora was leaning over at what appeared to be a very dangerous angle, her face precariously pasted up against the nothingness.

"Lenora! Careful! You'll fall!"

"No, I won't. Feel it and you'll see. It's like an invisible wall."

Coren put his hand out into the void. It bumped into something that was not there. Lenora was right.

"And," she added, "if you squint hard—well, there's something out there. I'm not sure what, but something."

Coren bent forward until his face touched the invisible something. Yes! There was something there—movements, colors maybe. It was very hard to make out.

"What do you think it could be?" he asked Lenora.

"I don't know. But look." Her hand trailing along the invisible wall, she was moving forward, brushing by a number of racks of coats. "It keeps going right along here behind all these coats until we come to the side wall."

"Do you think maybe it continues on the other side of that wall?"

"Good question. Let's go and look."

The place next door to all the hanging coats was yet another open-fronted room filled with racks and racks of objects labeled with numbers. This time, the objects were various cups and plates and balloons and stuffed toys and other small objects. Each and every one of the things in the room had the word *Winnipeg* on it. The people here certainly did love to write names on things—perhaps they had very bad memories and needed constant reminders of who and where they were.

Nodding to an older woman who sat behind a counter near the front, Lenora and Coren hurried down the aisles toward where the back wall ought to be. There were a number of colorful shirts there, all of them with the same saying printed on them: MY PARENTS WENT TO WINNIPEG, AND ALL I GOT WAS THIS LOUSY T-SHIRT. The shirts were hanging where a wall ought to be. But there was no wall. The shirts, pasted flatly against nothing, seemed to be floating in midair.

"It *does* continue," Lenora said.

"Can I help you with something?" said the woman from behind the counter. She had followed them and was now smiling broadly at them. "Like, one of these adorable T-shirts, maybe? Aren't they ever so sweet?"

"Can you tell me," Lenora said, getting straight to the point, "why there isn't a wall here?"

The woman seemed puzzled. "There isn't?"

"Well," Lenora asked her, "do *you* see one?"

"No, now that you mention it. Should there be?"

"Of course there should," Lenora said.

"And," Coren added, "if there isn't one, then why isn't there any snow out there, and why isn't it blowing in?"

The woman looked even more puzzled. Then she shook her head and smiled again. "It's always been like that, you know. Speaking of snow, can I interest you in a glass snow dome with a little miniature convention center in it? A perfect souvenir of your stay here, don't you think?"

Lenora was not about to be distracted. "It's always been like that? The wall, I mean."

"Well, yes."

"And have you always worked here?" Coren said, suddenly *very* interested in her answer.

"Why, yes. Always."

"Your whole life?" Coren persisted.

"Well, yes."

"So, even when you were small?"

"Small?" she said.

"A child?"

The woman looked puzzled. "Well, I wasn't . . . that is . . . of course, I see children but . . . I must have been . . ." The woman's words trailed off into silence. She looked more puzzled than ever.

Coren folded his arms and looked triumphantly at Lenora. "I thought so," he said.

"What?" she asked.

"She *wasn't* a child—not ever."

"That's silly, Coren, everybody starts off as a child. She must have been one, right?"

"Excuse me," the woman said, "I seem to be developing a bit of a headache—I'll go get myself something for it and be right back." She headed to the counter at the front without waiting for a reply.

"She wouldn't remember being a child if she had been created as an adult! And she says she's been doing this ever since she was created. She has no past, Lenora! No past at all!"

"Which means . . . ?"

"Which means that this place is somebody's creation! Sayley *must* have done it! And"—another thought struck him—"that place there, where the wall should be—that must be the edge of it, the end of the creation! That's why it stops like that. If we could just see what was out there . . ." He turned to the wall and peered out between a pair of T-shirts.

Sighing, Lenora followed. It was looking more and more like Sayley was to blame after all.

There was, Coren could see, something out there, way off in the distance. Shifting colors, like clouds, perhaps, or light sparkling on the surface of a pond.

Then, suddenly, something seemed to zoom down toward him out of the nothing, something huge and pinkish.

And in the middle of it was—an eye! Yes, a huge eye filled the entire wall, so that the colorful T-shirts seemed to float on it like gaudy dust motes.

A wave of dark brown points followed by more pinkish orange descended over the eye, hiding it momentarily—and then, just as quickly, retreated and revealed it again. And then the eye grew smaller, fuzzier, and disappeared altogether.

It was gone.

Chapter 13

"That was an eye, Coren! A giant eye!"

"Or" he said, remembering a fantasy book Lenora had lent him about a similar eye, "perhaps it was a regular-size eye. Perhaps it's we who are small."

"Don't be silly, Coren. I'm the same size I've always been— and so are you."

"But that's just it. If we stayed the same size in relation to each other—and in relation to everything else around us— well, we wouldn't even realize we'd got smaller, right?"

"I suppose so. But I don't feel small."

"Our being smaller would make sense of everything."

"It would?"

"Yes. It would. Think about it. We've decided that this place is probably somebody's creation—Sayley's, most likely. And what places have been created lately—lots of different places?"

"The exhibits!" Lenora realized, her mind racing. "The Meeting of Minds contest entries. And the exhibits are done in miniature, so that they'll all fit into the ballroom!"

"And for the same reason, remember, they all have edges—they're only allowed to occupy a certain amount of space. It's in the rules."

Lenora nodded.

"So if you were inside one of the exhibits," Coren said, "and you came to the edge and looked out, it would look just like this." He gestured to the wall of nothing in front of them.

"Much as I hate to admit it, Coren, you're right—you must be. We have somehow ended up in one of the contest entries."

"And obviously," he said sadly as he looked around the garish room, "it's one of the worst-possible-world exhibits."

"Obviously," she agreed. "These shirts here are just as nasty as those little books we found before. How could somebody be mean enough to actually give one to somebody? And to a child, at that! I couldn't imagine anything crueler."

"That seems to be the point—somebody sat down and imagined the cruelest, meanest thing they could—and created all this."

"And was cruel enough and mean enough to put us in it. I hate it, Coren. I want out."

"Me, too. But—"

"HELP!" she suddenly shouted at the top of her voice, cupping her hands around her mouth and pressing them against the nonexistent wall. "Get us out of here! I mean it! Whoever you are, we don't belong here! Get us out! Now! Now!"

The eye had been so big, and they, in comparison, were so small. And who knew how thick that invisible wall was, or how soundproof? Wasn't there something about soundproofing in the contest regulations? The chance of anyone out there actually hearing them was slight at best. But there didn't seem to be anything else to do.

"Release us!" Coren started to yell as he, too, pressed his face against the nothing. "Release us! Please! Somebody help!"

"Hey, youse guys," said a deep male voice behind him, "what's the problem here?"

Coren turned to look. It was a burly, dangerous-looking man in a dark blue uniform. SECURITY, it said on the front of his cap. Another Security.

Before he could think of anything to say, another voice interrupted. "Why, it's them! I told you they'd still be in here somewhere. Not that you were willing to drag yourself away from your precious doughnuts." It was the woman with the paper on her blouse that said SANDRA B.—the one who'd been sent to get Security earlier. She had bustled into the shop right on the heels of this new Security and was looking very annoyed.

"Listen, lady," the Security said to her, "I wasn't doing nothing wrong—it was my regulation break time, and I was just taking my break, is all. Jeez."

"Indeed? And what if a riot had broken out? I suppose you'd have gone right on scarfing down doughnuts anyway, with a complete and total disregard for public safety. What you don't seem to realize, sir, is that I am the one who invited those authors here—and you know how touchy authors are. This pair is even worse than most. Egos the size of Portage Place. And it's me they'd sue if anything happened to them, not you, Mr. Doughnut Man."

"Yeah, yeah," Security said. "Give it a rest, lady. Anyway, here they are now, right?"

"Right—as sheer luck would have it. Here they are. Arrest them."

"But, lady, I can't just—" He stopped in midsentence, distracted by the sound of breaking glass behind him.

"Run, Coren," Lenora shouted as she herself dashed for the

entrance. While Sandra B. and Security were busily engaged in conversation with each other, she had managed to pick up one of the snow domes from a shelf close by and toss it right over their heads and into a high stack of mugs, which immediately and very loudly crashed to the floor.

"My mugs!" the lady behind the counter shouted, rushing over and grabbing the security guard's arm. "My precious Winnipeg mugs! Do something!"

"Arrest them!" Sandra B. called, pulling on his other arm.

"Stop!" Security said, trying to wriggle out of their grasp. "They're getting away!"

By the time the three of them managed to extricate themselves from one another and make their way over the shattered mugs and out into the corridor, Lenora and Coren were no longer to be seen.

"Well," said Lenora as she watched the three disappear down the corridor, the two women screaming at Security as they went, "these coats were good for something after all." She stepped out from behind the rack. "Now what do we do?"

"Think. Figure out how to attract the attention of someone outside the exhibit who can get us out of here. You know, Lenora, when I get my hands on that little monster Sayley, I'm going to—"

"Sayley," Lenora mused. "*She's* outside, right? And those people back in the chapel seemed to think *they* could get her attention. They were actually praying to her. Do you think—?"

"Forget it," Coren said. "I am not praying to any nasty-minded little ten-year-old girl, and that's that. Still—the chapel's not a bad idea. It's sort of off the beaten track, and the people there are the only ones we've met all day who haven't tried to get Security after us."

"Perhaps," Lenora said with a teasing smile, "it's the civilizing influence of that nasty-minded ten-year-old?"

"Ho, ho. Very funny. Anyway, those people aren't going to spend all day in that ridiculous ceremony. And once they're gone, we can have the place to ourselves."

Sure enough, the first thing Lenora and Coren heard after they snuck through the corridors and opened the door of the chapel was the crowd all chanting together, "Let us go now in peace!"

"But," the man at the pulpit added, "let us not forget our better selves. Let us not forget to invite Sayley into our lives! Sayley be with us."

"Sayley be with us!" the crowd repeated.

"Sayley!" said King Arno. "There you are. Come here! Join us over here at the refreshment table and have one of my cinnamon buns."

But Sayley was too worried to think about cinnamon buns. She stared at her own creation.

It was them. She was almost sure it was them. Coren and Lenora, inside her creation. Catching a glimpse of them in there had been a terrible shock, because she had just passed Lenora and Coren in the corridor a few moments ago, so it couldn't *really* be them. No, it must be just a couple of the people she had imagined who dressed up like Lenora and Coren.

Nevertheless, this pair really did look like Lenora and Coren, down to the smallest detail—and none of the would-be Lenoras and Corens she'd invented were supposed to look anything much like the originals at all. They wanted to, but they had so little faith in the possibilities of their imaginations that they never quite managed to bring it off, so that what they imagined simply didn't happen, at least not as completely or realistically as they hoped. Surely she hadn't slipped up somehow and put those two very successful imitators in there?

Because they were uncomfortably successful, no question about it. The way the Lenora was screaming, that trademark awful mad look on her face—that would be hard for anyone else to do.

Sayley shut her eyes, hoping the imitators would go away, and then opened them again. The two of them were still there, jumping up and down and shouting at her as if, somehow, they actually knew she was there and they were furious with her.

That was simply impossible. She had been *sure* to create only people who would like where they were living, who wouldn't think there was anything much the matter with it. To do anything else would have been terribly cruel. Why, she'd even arranged it so that the people would actually want to thank their creator for creating them and their world—even though, of course, they were so devoid of imaginative power that they could never quite believe the creator really existed, since they could never actually see her or have contact with her. Her creations would never actually *shout* at her.

But these two seemed to be doing just that. She could hear their anger even through the thick soundproof walls required by the contest regulations. Muffled, but still audible.

Well, then, maybe it *was* Lenora and Coren. Maybe Lenora had decided to put herself in there, just for fun, perhaps, or to tease Coren the way she often did, and then, had been unable to get the two of them out?

Because that was one thing Sayley was sure about. Once in there, even Lenora could not imagine herself out. That was the whole thing about that creation—what made it so truly awful, what had led the judges to award it first prize in its category for worst possible world and send it on to the adult exhibition. In it, imagination was just fantasy—no matter how much people wished or hoped, it never ever became real, because despite their wishes, the people didn't actually believe it was possible for it to be real. It was pure genius, Sayley thought. Not even Lenora's powerful imagination would work down there.

But, Sayley told herself, her own might. She had created it, after all. Quickly, she closed her eyes and imagined the two figures—now involved in some kind of conversation with a security guard and the officious book lady she had modeled on her horrible Aunt Sarndina—out of there and in the exhibit hall beside her.

She opened her eyes. Nothing. They were still there, arguing with the other two.

Sayley's heart began to race. She had somehow managed to create an environment more powerfully unimaginative than her own strong imagination. *That* was dangerous—and she knew she was going to have to tell people about it. Lenora's and Coren's parents would be furious with her—not to mention her own parents. They might even take away her first prize. It wasn't fair, it simply wasn't fair at all.

"You see," she heard a familiar voice say from behind her, "everything is exactly the way it should be." She turned to see Lenora, there in the exhibit hall.

So it wasn't her down there in the creation after all. Thank heavens for that at least.

Still, the Lenora down there—she and the Coren with her were now making a terrible mess of Sayley's adorable shop full of things that had that wonderfully awful name Winnipeg on them, as if it were a name people might want to remember—looked much too much like the real Lenora to make Sayley happy. The real Lenora must have had something to do with it. Maybe she was just teasing Sayley somehow, controlling

Sayley's imagination with her own so that Sayley couldn't get the duplicate out of there. Sayley decided to follow Lenora and Coren to see if she could discover anything.

Lenora was speaking to a group of guests from Grag—a number of fairies, some elves, and a troll. It seemed she was showing off her own contribution to the exhibit. In the excitement of having her own creations on display, Sayley hadn't yet had a chance to look at Lenora's, which was bound to be truly wild. Thank goodness Lenora's creations were in the adult category, or else Sayley would never have won any praise at all. Sayley moved a little closer to take a look at the exhibit and began to eavesdrop.

"In fact," Lenora was saying, "it's almost exactly like the world we have now. I did make a few important adjustments. For instance, everybody understands the importance of color matching in both home decoration and personal attire, and even the simplest of rural bumpkins lives by a high standard of tasteful elegance. But otherwise I haven't changed a thing. After all, we *already* have the perfect Balance, don't we?"

As Lenora smiled, paused, and waited for the Gragians to agree with her, Sayley stared at her. The perfect Balance? A world just like this one? It was wrong, all wrong. Lenora never thought *anything* was perfect. She was always creating better worlds, imagining different things, making trouble, in fact. Just like Sayley herself.

"Lenora," Sayley interrupted as the Gragians smiled and moved off, shaking their heads in confusion at this uncharacteristic behavior in their old friend, "this isn't your *real* vision is it?" Sayley looked down at the surprisingly lackluster exhibit in disbelief—it truly was just like the real world already was, except everybody wore intricately designed clothes, as if that was their only interest. Since when did Lenora care about *fashion*?

"Or maybe this is your *worst* world vision? Is that what it is?"

Lenora glared at her. "What's wrong with it?" she demanded.

"It's boring, of course," Sayley said. "It's just like this world but with different outfits. Really! I mean, don't *you* think it's boring?"

"Boring!" Lenora snapped. She gestured around the hall. "No, certainly not. If you ask me, it's all these other weird ideas that are boring. Aren't they, Cor—uh, Coren?"

Coren was standing beside Lenora, peculiar looks darting wildly across his face that suggested he was totally caught up in his thoughts. Every once in a while he would grab at his hip—where a sword would be hanging if he were wearing a sword, which he wasn't, of course, because he never did. Then he would look confused for a moment, nod a little, and go back to whatever it was he was thinking about.

When he didn't respond to her words, Lenora jabbed him in the side, at which he immediately went for the nonexistent sword again, then looked confused, nodded again, and said, "Whatever you say, Len—I mean, Lenora."

"Truly and completely boring," Lenora continued before he had even finished speaking. "Worlds where ruffles are outlawed! Worlds where no one ever thinks about what they're wearing! Worlds without any clothes at all!"

"Actually," Coren said, giving Lenora a defiant look, "I rather like that one."

"Oh, Coren, of course you don't." She jabbed his side again. "Do you?"

"Oof!" he said, once more reaching for the nonexistent sword and then staring unhappily at his empty hand. "Well, Len—I mean, Lenora, when you come to think of it, I guess, it really doesn't leave much scope for concealed weapons."

"Of course it doesn't. And how would you know who was who? Why, the maids would look just like the princesses! You'd have to treat everybody the same! Have people taken total leave of their senses?"

The look of horror on Lenora's face seemed, Sayley decided, totally sincere. She really did not like any of the new, innovative ideas that filled the hall. Something was *very* wrong. This was *not* Lenora speaking.

And why did Coren keep putting his hand to his belt as if to search for a sword? Coren was a cowardly wimp. He never carried a sword if he could possibly help it. He never got within ten feet of a sword if he could possibly help it.

And wait a minute—wasn't there something wrong with the way Coren looked? Although he was wearing a loose, wide-sleeved top that hid his shape, he seemed less skinny than usual, more muscular.

More like Cori, Coren's look-alike, who spent hours every day lifting weights and admiring the results in a mirror. And Cori carried a sword at all times, even while lifting weights, even (so he claimed) while bathing, in case of intruders—he was always going on about how that was why he insisted on a rustproof finish on all his swords. And Cori's fiancée, Leni—well, Sayley would bet that Leni's feelings about the displays would be *exactly* what this so-called Lenora was busy spouting. And under the makeup she always wore Leni looked *exactly* like Lenora. If she left off the makeup . . .

Unlike those poor, deluded fools Sayley had crated for her exhibit, in fact, Leni and Cori looked almost *exactly* like Lenora and Coren.

"Aha!" Sayley said out loud. "Of course! I should have known!"

"Known what?" said the person who looked exactly like Lenora, eyeing her suspiciously.

"You're Leni! And you're Cori!"

## Chapter 14

"Me? Leni?

"Me? Cori?"

They both laughed loudly. But the look on their faces told Sayley she was right.

"You are them! You are Leni and Cori!"

"Oh, Cori," Leni said, stamping her foot. "This child is far too annoying."

"If only I had my sword," Cori said, eyes glaring at Sayley as he grasped ineffectually at his hip. "I'd rip her from stem to stern!"

*Just try it, mister, and see what happens*, Sayley thought grimly.

"Indeed?" Cori said to her, a belligerent gleam in his eye. "What *will* happen?"

*Rats*, Sayley told herself, *I forgot Cori could read my thoughts*.

"Well, I can," Cori said. "And I don't like what I'm reading there, little girl. What you are thinking isn't the least bit lady-like." Suddenly his face changed and his cheeks colored a little.

"*That*, in particular," he told her, "*that* was a very unladylike thing for you to think. And, anyway, I suspect, physically impossible."

"Perhaps," Sayley said in a menacing voice that actually made him cringe, "but that doesn't mean I couldn't try, does it? Why are you two pretending to be Lenora and Coren?"

Leni gave her a haughty look. "What business is it of yours, I'd like to know? You're just an insignificant little girl. You don't even have noble blood. We don't have to tell *you* anything."

"Lenora and Coren are my friends," Sayley said, furious. "You had no business putting them in that horrible world I invented! Oh, I know you did it, because I saw them in there, so there's no point in denying it. But *why*? Why did you do it?"

"Well," replied Leni, "it's obvious, isn't it? Lenora is *such* a troublemaker. Always changing the Balance. Always creating havoc. Why, she can't even match up a skirt and top, not if her life depended on it! And if you ask me, she has absolutely *no* concept of good hair. Not any."

"You sent Lenora off because she has no fashion sense?" Sayley squeaked.

Leni didn't even hear her. "But of course," she continued, "Mother and Father always prefer her. I don't know *why*, because I'm the good one. I'm the one who always listens. And *she* does nothing but make trouble. Who knows what might have happened to our dear, old wonderful world if *she* had any say about who won the contest? I mean, honestly!" Leni paused, a strange smile moving across her lips. "You know what I think? I think that actually they'll *all* be glad to be rid of Lenora—especially Mother and Father. They just don't know it yet."

"You've taken complete leave of your senses!" Sayley said.

She couldn't believe what she was hearing. *And,* she thought, *I'd better hurry up and tell Lenora's parents. We have to get her back here.*

"You won't tell her parents," Cori said, his hand once more reaching for his nonexistent sword. "My Leni has a good plan, and you, young whippersnapper, are *not* going to ruin it!"

"And just how do you plan to stop me?" Sayley said, hands on hips. "In fact, there's Queen Milda now. Your Highness," she called. "Please, may I talk to you? It's urgent!"

Queen Milda hurried over. "Oh hello, Lenora, Coren," she said as she approached them, her head darting around as if searching for someone. "You're looking very well today, Coren—very healthy. Have you put on some weight? It must be love. Anyway, I thought Sayley was calling me. Wasn't she just here? I could have sworn—"

"Sayley?" said Leni. "That adorable little girl from the country? I haven't seen her all day. Have we, Coren?" She gave him a jab in the side.

"Uh, no," said Cori. "Not all day. How are *you* today, Mother? Supplies of dragon not running short, by any chance?"

"With that peculiar boy Cori slaying dragons all the time? Not a chance." She stopped talking and began sending her thoughts mind to mind. *I tell you, Coren dear, it takes a muscle-bound ninny like that to make me appreciate how lucky I am to have a son like you. The poor dear hasn't a brain in his thick skull!*

*I do so!* he thought back. His mother looked puzzled. Leni realized that he must be giving her the wrong answer and gave him another jab. "Uh . . . I mean, yes, Mother, you're right," he said aloud.

*Of course I am, Coren,* she thought back. She gave him a big smile. *I'm always right—didn't I find this wonderful girl for you?* She gave Leni a quick, affectionate squeeze, then said aloud,

"Anyway, my dears, I must dash. The Nefarion exhibit has given me a few new ideas for my own creation—hot and cold running water in every tree! I'm going to get that dear man, Nobelwarm, to imagine it into my exhibit for me right now. He's your uncle, isn't he, Lenora? You Gepethians are so handy!"

As the queen hurried off Cori, once more grabbing at his hip, looked wildly around.

"Where is she?" he said. "Where did the little brat get to? I tell you, Leni, throttling isn't good enough for her."

"Oh," said Leni with a strangely placid smile, "I don't think we have to worry about *her* anymore."

"We don't?"

"Come and see." She took his hand and guided him over to Sayley's worst-world exhibit. "Just take a little peek in there."

He bent over and looked in to where Leni was pointing. It seemed to be some sort of gathering—little people all together in a small, bleak-looking room with a picture of a sunset on the wall. Most of them were looking at a smaller group and seemed to be shouting angrily at them.

There were three figures in the smaller group. Familiar-looking figures. He looked more closely. Lenora. Coren. And, yes! The miserable little brat. Leni had imagined Sayley into the exhibit, right along with Lenora and Coren.

"See," Leni said in a triumphant voice. "All the trouble-makers in one place—a place they can't get out of no matter how hard they try! Sayley is gone—gone for good!"

Chapter 15

"Let Sayley be here!" the crowd in the chapel had been chanting enthusiastically. "Here for good! Here for the good of us all! Let the Divine Presence be with us!"

That was when Lenora had heard a loud ripping noise. It came from the square of white material at the front. Lenora looked up to see it tear right down the middle, cleaving the face of the Divine Sayley in half.

Except that the face had remained somehow, despite the rip. Or rather, there was another face there, a giant face that had been hidden behind the first one and was exposed through the rip. It was similar to the first face but lacked the serenity. In fact, it seemed terrified. It looked to Lenora exactly the way the real Sayley would look if she were frightened out of her wits.

"Nooooooooooo!" the giant face had screamed, and even as it screamed it had appeared to be diminishing, growing smaller by the second. Finally it was no larger than life-size, small enough for Lenora to see that there was a normal-size body attached to it. Sayley's body, attached to Sayley's face, suspended in midair in front of the chapel. Then, with a painfully loud crash, it fell to the floor. It was lying there now.

"Sayley!" Lenora exclaimed as she ran toward the fallen figure. "Are you okay?"

Sayley lifted her head from the floor, looking more than a little dazed. "Lenora? Coren? It is you, isn't it?"

"Yes, of course it is," said Lenora anxiously. "That was quite a tumble you took. What happened?"

"Well," Sayley began, "I was—"

"Very cute," said an angry voice. It was the man in the red wig and black suit who was standing behind the pulpit. "Very funny."

The rest of the crowd, who had been watching in shocked silence, began to nod and mumble. "Disgraceful," they said.

"I beg your pardon?" Lenora had no idea what the man was going on about. Couldn't he see the poor child might be hurt?

"I said," the man continued, "that it was a clever bit of magic, or whatever it was. Making the child appear out of nowhere like that—and just at the appropriate moment, too. Why, for a second there, I might almost have believed that—" He stopped in midsentence and his face grew even angrier. "Oh yes, very clever, making fun of other people's beliefs. Very mature indeed." The crowd murmured louder.

"But," Lenora began, "we didn't—"

"But nothing," the angry man interrupted. "You teenagers today"—he looked out at the crowd—"I exclude, of course, all you fine young folk who have found room for Sayley in your busy lives. But"—he looked again at Lenora and Coren with deep loathing—"as for you others. You have no respect, for anyone, no morals, no manners, no hygiene, no spiritual values. Personally, I blame the educational system. And what

I want to know is, who's going to pay for it? Replacing that screen you destroyed is going to cost, and cost big. And it's certainly not going to be me—or, if I have anything to do with it, any of the good young folk who gathered here today to celebrate their spiritual life."

There were yet more murmurs of agreement from the crowd.

"Now, just a minute," Coren found himself saying as he jumped to his feet—he was much angrier than he had realized. "Don't you have any compassion at all? Why, poor Sayley here—"

"Sayley," the man interrupted. "Sayley indeed! How dare you call that unfortunate excuse for a child by the name of the Divine Sayley? Surely you are not going to persist in this wretched little charade, are you? Because I assure you, it is rapidly beginning to lose whatever very tiny bit of humor it ever had. That scruffy little underage female is not anything like the Divine Sayley. Praise her."

"Praise her," the crowd repeated.

Now Sayley was on her feet and raging. "How dare you?" she said. "How dare you call me scruffy? I created you, and I can uncreate you whenever I want to, so you'd better watch your step!" Her eyes shot daggers at him.

The crowd drew in their breath as one and stared at her.

Finally, the man behind the pulpit spoke. "This has gone too far," he said, quivering in rage. "This is sacrilege! You people are sick, just plain sick. Somebody call for security."

*Oh no*, Coren thought. *Here we go again.* Quickly, he grabbed Sayley's trembling hand and began to pull her toward the door. "That won't be necessary," he said over his shoulder. "We apologize for any trouble we might have caused. And we'll just get out of your way. Right now. Come along, Sayley. Come along, Lenora."

"Wait!" the man shouted. "The screen! Don't let them go. Somebody catch them."

But it was too late. Coren had already dragged Sayley through the door, Lenora following closely behind her.

"So much for our last refuge," he said, looking nervously behind him. "They'll be after us any second now. Where to?"

"The coats!" Lenora said. It was the only place she could think of where they could hide. And so, once more, they found themselves huddled behind rows of coats, desperately hoping that none of their growing army of pursuers had seen which way they came. For the moment, at least, they seemed to be safe.

"Sayley dear," said Lenora, "I think you have some explaining to do."

Sayley's body suddenly grew rigid and her eyes blazed. "I'll kill those two!" she said. "I will! If you won't get rid of them, Lenora, I will. Oh, this is horrible! This is awful! We'll *never* get out of here!" And she started to cry.

"Sayley," Lenora implored her, "crying won't help, will it? You have to calm down and tell us what is going on. *Which* two will you kill? Who are you talking about? What has happened?"

"It's Cori and Leni. It was Leni who put you in here, and then she—"

"Leni!" Coren interrupted, shaking his head ruefully. "I suppose we should have known."

Leni was perfectly capable of imagining him and Lenora in here if she wanted to—and apparently, she had wanted to.

It was strange that she wanted to—totally untypical of her. What could have happened to Leni to make her desert her obsessive concern with the status quo? Could her envy of Lenora actually be that strong? He and Lenora were certainly going to have to be more considerate toward the poor girl—if they ever did manage to get back home again.

"But," Lenora was saying to Sayley, "surely Leni didn't imagine this place? It's much too . . . well, too *interesting* for her."

Sayley's sad face brightened a little. "Yes, it is interesting, isn't it? It's mine! It's one of my exhibits for the contest."

Coren nodded. "I told you so, Lenora."

"Shush, Coren. Let Sayley tell us about it. Go ahead, dear."

"Well," Sayley continued, "I created this place as my worst possible world, see?" She popped her head up from the coats and took an admiring glance around. "And I did a really good job, too! It's even better close up!"

*Depends,* Coren thought, *on what you mean by 'better.'* For one thing, she might have gone a little lighter on Security. And the snow. And as for all those pretend versions of himself with their ridiculous painted-on freckles—

"The judges agree, too," Sayley went on. "I won first prize in the youth division!"

"Good for you, Sayley!" Lenora said.

"The judges said I had a truly despicable mind! Isn't that great? Anyway, I was bending down and looking at the exhibit when I saw you two there! It wasn't my fault, Lenora, honest! It was Leni who did it. And"—her eyes grew large—"do you know why?"

"Why?" Lenora asked.

"Because she's pretending to be you! She's taken your place!"

That, Coren told himself, wasn't particularly surprising either. In recent days Leni had been growing increasingly jealous of all the attention Lenora was getting as the wedding day approached. And with Lenora out of the way—

"Leni's going around saying she's you," Sayley continued breathlessly, "and no one has even noticed—too busy thinking about themselves, I guess. But not me! I noticed! And I confronted her, too, and she admitted it! And so"—her face changed and her voice disappeared into a barely audible mumble—"so she put me in here, too. And now we're stuck here in the worst place in all the worlds! We're stuck in Winnipeg forever!" Sayley began to cry again.

Lenora patted her hand and looked at Coren over her head.

"But, Sayley," he said, "surely it isn't as bad as all that. Lenora is just as powerful as Leni, don't forget. And so are you, almost. If Leni can imagine us in here, then Lenora and you together can certainly imagine us out again."

It seemed logical, Lenora told herself—although, she remembered, she herself had not been able to manage it earlier. But Coren was right. Sayley's imagination was indeed almost as powerful as her own. Maybe—

"Maybe," she said, "Sayley and I *can* do it together. Come on, Sayley. Hold my hand and imagine that we're out of here."

They did. They shut their eyes and imagined, as hard as they could, that they were back in the palace in Andilla.

They opened their eyes. They were still crouched behind the coats.

"I knew it wouldn't work," Sayley said gloomily. "Oh, it's my fault, it's all my fault." She sniffled.

"No, Sayley," said Lenora, patting her consolingly. "It was Leni who—"

"But I was the one who made it so that our powers wouldn't work."

"You did?"

"Yes, I did. See, when I was thinking about making an entry for the contest, I tried to imagine the worst possible thing that could be. And I thought about Mudd and the rest of the Skwoes."

Coren nodded. He himself had seen more than enough of the Skwoes, a group of people who had, until recently, lived secretly in the Andillan countryside and who were completely devoid of any imagination whatsoever. Mudd, the boy with whom Sayley had had a number of run-ins, was a decidedly typical Skwoe, as practical as they come.

"I said to myself," Sayley continued, "what would be even worse than being a Skwoe? And then it came to me! What if you did have an imagination but you didn't actually believe in it?"

Lenora looked puzzled. "I'm not sure I—"

"It's simple! I made this world really terrible—did you see any of that awful snow I put in?"

Lenora and Coren nodded.

"Isn't it truly dreadful? I made all that stuff, and then I created these people in here so that their minds could invent all sorts of wonderful possibilities about different places and all—places without snow or shopping malls or chicken that tasted like cardboard. But—and this is the genius part, Lenora!—I made them so that they would never actually believe in their own imaginations! Because they don't believe, they can't actually make anything they imagine real! Isn't that awful? Isn't it neat?"

"But Sayley," Coren said, trying to think this all through, "why did you put *us* in this world? Me and Lenora. Not the *real* us. . . . I mean, all those people who were pretending to be us—the ones who think we're just characters in books."

"Don't you get it? It's because they don't trust their imaginations. They love the idea that people like us exist—that's why they read books, and why I wrote us into the books for them to read. But they can't believe it's really possible. They think these silly authors I created just made us up. So they just play at believing it—dressing up like actors and pretending to be us and knowing all along they can't be anything but what they already are and that reality can't be anything but what it already is. Pathetic, right?"

There was a time when Coren would have disagreed, when he wanted nothing but reality as it already was. But now, after his adventures with Lenora . . . Well, Sayley was right in a way. It was sort of pathetic. And it certainly accounted for why everyone refused to believe that he and Lenora were who they said they were. No wonder they all kept calling for Security.

"And," Sayley added miserably, "that's why we can't ever get out of here! Everyone in here believes that imaginative powers like ours and countries like Gepeth and Andilla are just fantasies—and so, in here, they *are* just fantasies. We can't get back to Andilla because no one here really believes it could exist. Why, even those people back there in the chapel who came to worship me—it was silly of me to get mad at them, because even *they* don't believe I could exist, not really. They think I'm just symbolic or something. We're doomed! We're stuck here forever!"

## Chapter 16

"It's not your fault, Sayley," Lenora said. "You couldn't have known that Leni would actually decide to do something besides fiddle with her hair for a change. Blast her, anyway. If I ever get my hands on her—"

"Not if I get to her first," said Sayley, gritting her teeth. She peeked out through the coats. "I sure would like to see more of this place. It isn't often you get a chance to actually be inside your own creation."

Coren glared at her. But before he could say anything, Lenora nodded. "I know what you mean, Sayley," she said. "Detail work is so hard, especially on this scale. It *is* a wonderful opportunity."

"What I'd really like to see," Sayley said, "is Portage Place. It's so neat! You have to trade dirty colored papers for the things you want! Have you been there?"

Lenora nodded.

"Isn't it terrible?" Sayley said gleefully. "Did you notice how all the shoes and hats and things are all just a teensy bit different from each other? It makes the people think they need new things all the time, even if the old ones aren't worn out!"

Lenora looked at Sayley and shook her head. "It worries me," Lenora said, "that someone so young could think up something so awful."

"I got the idea from Leni," Sayley said. "You know how she's always going on about how wide her pleats should be and whether her hair should be shorter or longer. I thought that if I just made the kind of place *she* would like, it would end up being truly horrible. I'd certainly *love* to see more of it." She gave Lenora a pleading look.

"No!" Coren exclaimed. "We can't! It isn't safe! Everyone is out to get us! Security—"

"Now, Coren," Lenora interrupted. "We can't stay here forever. We still have to figure out a way to get out of here—and looking around a little may give us an idea. Who knows, maybe Sayley will remember something she put in here that will help."

"I suppose so," he said grudgingly. "But if Security ever—"

It was too late. Lenora had already pushed aside the coats and headed off down the corridor, Sayley rushing along behind her. "Come on, Coren," Lenora shouted over her shoulder. "Don't be a slowpoke."

Sighing, Coren headed off after them—they had already turned a corner and disappeared from view. By the time he caught up with them, they were standing stock still, staring out across the large open space near the door to the outside.

"Coren!" Lenora said. "Look—it's *them* again! Heading right this way!"

"Carol!" the male author standing just in front of her echoed. "Look—it's *them* again! Heading right this way!"

The two authors were bundled up in heavy coats and hats. They must have been on their way out of the convention building.

"Oh, no," groaned Carol M. "Not you two again. And"—she glanced at Sayley—"now you have a child with you."

"Sayley, no doubt," said Perry N., his voice reeking of sarcasm as he looked anxiously around to see if help was available.

Sayley beamed. "Good for you! I made you quite clever, didn't I?" She held up her hand and shook her head a little, still smiling. "Don't thank me. Just watching you work is reward enough!"

"Carol," Perry N. said anxiously, "they really *are* deranged. Let's get out of here." He turned and began to head for the door.

"Good heavens," Lenora said, exasperated. "I don't believe this! We aren't going to *hurt* you!" Perry N. gave her another frightened look and took a few extra steps back.

"Although," Sayley said, "I can see why they might worry about that. I did put a lot of senseless violence into this world, Lenora."

"*You* did?" Carol M. asked. Now it was her turn to look suspicious and uneasy.

"Well, yes, of course," Sayley said. "And I can understand how that might make you distrustful. But we'd never hurt you. You are my creations, after all!"

"That does it," said Perry N. All the fear had left his voice, and he glared at Sayley. "That takes the cake. Messing around with our signing is bad enough, not to mention stealing our books. I mean, do you think we writers live on air?"

"Now, Perry—," Carol M. began.

"Carol," he interrupted, "you know as well as I do that we could never write anything at all if everybody just went around like these two reading our books for free! How would we even get the money to buy the things we need? I myself *desperately* need a pair of no-skid ice runners, and they're so expensive! And then . . . then . . . as if that weren't bad enough, this nasty little brat has the chutzpah to call these two Lenora and Coren again, and to say that she is the *real* Sayley to whom we all must pray. Honestly!"

"But," said Sayley, "they *are* Lenora and Coren. And I *am* Sayley."

"Oh, you are, are you?" Perry N. said scornfully. "So what do we do, then, O Divine Sayley? Get down on our knees before you? I mean, it's not every day you get to meet your creator, is it?"

"I know!" Sayley answered, excited. "It's not every day you get to meet your creations, either! This is amazing! But there's no need to bow—unless you really want to."

Carol M. looked at Perry N. and shook her head. "Don't encourage her," Carol M. scolded. "She's only a child, and see how deluded she is? She needs help."

"Help?" said Sayley. "Oh, yes, help! I forgot! I *did* put in a whole group of people whose only job is to think they know what's wrong with everyone else's minds and go around trying to fix them up whether they want it or not, all the while telling them they are helping them. Right! I need help! That's great!"

"See?" said Carol M., looking very distressed.

"Sayley," Coren reproved her. "Please. You're just making it worse. Let me speak to them."

"It's just so . . . so . . . fascinating, Coren," Sayley said. "I want to ask them so many things. Like, for instance," she turned to Perry N., "how do you like your special underwear?"

"Underwear?" Perry N. looked totally flabbergasted. "How could you possibly know about . . . I mean . . . never mind." He turned even brighter red than Coren usually got.

Coren nodded. "Never mind about the underwear. I mean, I'm sure, Sayley, that it's wonderful underwear."

"It is," she declared. "Wonderful. If you could just see it, Coren, it has—"

"Never!" Perry N. shrieked. "Never in a million years!" He clutched his coat tightly around him. "I *hate* these conventions!"

Watching Perry N.'s embarrassment, Coren suddenly had an idea. If Perry N. could accept that Sayley knew about his underwear—well, what if they could get the authors to accept that the three of them were really who they said they were? They were authors, after all, weren't they? And they thought they had created him and Lenora and Sayley. Who else would be more likely to believe in their reality? If the authors believed, even for a moment, maybe it would allow Lenora and Sayley to imagine them back home.

"I know it's hard," Coren said to Perry N., "but if you could only, just for *one* second, if you could consider or possibly, perhaps, imagine that Sayley *did* create all this—"

"Of course she did," Perry N. said, clutching his coat even more tightly and looking at Coren as if he were totally deranged. "Sayley *is* our creator, after all."

"It worked," Coren said, excited. "Quickly, Lenora, think about Andilla!"

"But," Perry N. went on, "this nasty little demon is certainly not *her*."

*Rats*, Coren thought, his hopes sinking.

"My underwear, of all things!" Perry N. continued. "Honestly! And anyway, Sayley is beyond mere underwear. She is so great as to be indescribable! She is everywhere and nowhere!"

"Even," Sayley muttered again, "in your underwear."

"Sayley made all and minds all!" Carol M. added happily. "Praise Sayley!" She turned to Perry. "What's all this about your underwear?"

"I'm confused," said Lenora. "In your book you write about a Sayley, a little child. Well, isn't that the same Sayley you pray to?"

"*You* pray to?" asked Carol M., confused. "Don't *you* pray to Sayley? Surely you're not one of those *awful* agnostics? I myself may not be religious, but I am very spiritual."

"Agnostics? Uh, no, of course not. Praise Sayley."

"Thank you, Lenora," said Sayley.

"I just wonder," Lenora said, "about why the girl in the book has that name."

"Oh," said Carol M. "Well, it was a joke, really. One of Perry's jokes, and not a very funny one, either."

"*I* think it's funny," said Perry N. "I mean, giving a dangerous little brat who can imagine strange worlds into existence the same name as the divine creator of our real world—it's cute!"

"Maybe," said Carol M. in an unconvinced voice. "But it's also sacrilegious. It's a wonder some of the clergy haven't started to attack us for it."

"Don't worry about it, Carol M.," Sayley said. "They won't. They also think it's just a harmless joke, and always will, I guarantee it. I made them know the Divine Sayley is above all that."

"Oh, she is, is she?" said Lenora, hands on hips, glaring at Sayley. "I can't believe you actually made yourself a *god*!"

Sayley looked a little abashed. "Well," she said with a little defiance, "I *did* create them, didn't I?"

"That's no excuse to have them worship you," Lenora scolded her.

"But it was fun!"

"Sayley! Honestly!"

Coren thought the sight of Lenora lecturing Sayley on an abuse of power was quite funny. Still, he tried to steer the conversation back to the authors, who were looking more nervous and upset than ever—if Security had been in sight, they would be shouting for him for sure.

"Never mind them," he said to Carol M. and Perry N., "they're just joking. Really. Listen to me. What if it *is* true? I mean, just for a second, consider it. How can you be *sure* it isn't? Please, please! If you would believe us for just a minute, maybe we could go back to Andilla."

"Yes," said Lenora, who now, finally, understood what Coren was trying to do. "Try!" She turned to Coren. "Good thinking," she said.

Sayley, however, shook her head. "It won't work," she insisted. "Not with these two. They don't have enough imagination— that's why it takes two of them to make up their books instead of just one."

"You *can't* go back to Andilla," said Carol M., now looking really frightened, her voice a high-pitched whine. "Andilla doesn't exist! We made it up! We made it all up! There is no Coren and no Lenora and no Andilla!"

"I've had enough, Carol," Perry N. said. "I mean, fans are fans, but my underwear is nobody's business but my own. Let's call security."

"See?" Sayley sighed. "They can't believe."

"Oh! Thank goodness!" a voice interrupted. "I thought I'd missed you!" It was a young boy, talking as he tried to gulp down air. He was a couple of years older than Sayley, with brown hair, pale, almost white skin, and pale blue eyes that could barely be seen through his fogged-up round glasses.

Sayley stared at the boy, shocked. *I'd forgotten all about him,* she thought. *How* could *I forget about him? And just look—he's as adorable as I imagined.*

"It is you, isn't it?" the boy continued. "Carol M. and Perry N.? The authors?"

"Yes," said Carol M., "it's us, but—"

"It's the storm that did it," the boy continued, still panting heavily as he removed his glasses and wiped them on his coat. "The bus was late, and it was so slow, we almost got stuck twice, and then I had to run all the way from The Gulf! But it was worth it! You're still here!" Eyes shining, the boy held up worn copies of the two small books Coren and Lenora had taken earlier. "They're my absolute favorites! I've read both books *six* times! I was wondering if you'd autograph them for me?"

"We'd really like to," Carol M. said, still staring apprehensively at Coren, "but—"

"But nothing," Perry N. said, grabbing Carol M. by the arm. "Let's get out of here now, Carol, while we can!" He began to pull Carol M. away. "Sorry," he said to the boy, "but the signing's over. Maybe next time."

"Now, just you listen here, Mr. Author!" It was Lenora. She had grabbed the back of Perry N.'s coat and made him turn around. "This boy wants you to write your name in his books, and you're going to do it! Right now! Or else! And don't even *think* of calling for Security, or the entire world will be seeing your underwear!"

Perry N. just looked at Lenora a moment, horror all over his face. Carol M.'s face matched his. Then, without saying a word, the two of them reached into their coats, took out their pens, and signed the books—although they were trembling so much that it was unlikely the signatures were the least bit legible.

"Good," said Lenora when they had finished. "You can go now."

"But Lenora," said Coren, "they still might—"

"Let's face it, Coren," she said. "It's useless. Sayley was right. They have no imagination! None at all!"

"Now, just a minute," said Carol M. "How dare you—?"

"Carol," Perry N. said, "they said we could go. Let's go. Now!" And with that he unceremoniously grabbed on to her arm and pulled her toward the door and out into the snow beyond.

"I wish I'd made them smarter," Sayley said, shaking her head as she watched them disappear into the white. "And I wish I'd made their underwear out of red-hot iron." It was a fervent wish. Now that they were gone, this adorable boy . . . well, it would all come out. What she'd done. She looked at the boy and felt herself blushing again.

# Chapter 17

"They did it!" the boy said, gazing happily at the books. "They actually signed them! 'Best wishes from our two minds to yours, Carol M. and' . . . I guess this scribble here says 'Perry N.'" His eyes shining, he turned to Lenora. "Thank you! Thank you so much for helping me get these, because I love the books so much and it means so much to—" Suddenly he stopped and gasped, staring hard at Lenora. "I don't believe it!" he said. Then he turned and gazed at Coren, then at Sayley. "And you, too! And you! *Especially* you! Those eyes! You look *exactly* like the real Lenora, the real Coren, and especially the real Sayley! Exactly the way I'd pictured them all in my mind, anyway. It is totally, truly, amazing!"

"You know," said Lenora, smiling gratefully at him, "you are the first person we've met here who wasn't too pigheaded to—" She paused and looked at the boy with hungry eyes. "Coren! Sayley! He thinks we look like us! Do you think maybe—?"

"It's worth a try," Coren said, excited. He turned to the boy.

"You actually think that we look like Coren and Lenora and Sayley? I mean, really?"

"Yes," the boy said. "You really do."

"Well, then," Coren continued. "I mean, I know this may sound silly, but could you possibly, even for the briefest of instants, could you, in fact, imagine that we, in fact, really—"

"Oh, for heaven's sake!" It was Sayley, and she sounded absolutely furious. "I can't stand it anymore. Let's get this whole silly business over with, right now. Yes, Coren, he *can* imagine it." She turned to the boy. "You can, can't you? Well, can't you?"

The boy looked very confused. "I . . . I don't understand—"

"Of course you do," Sayley spat at him. "You really do believe that Coren and Lenora and I are not just characters in books, right? You believe that it's not just fantasy and that we actually do exist. Right?"

The boy stared at her, looking completely mortified. "That's ridiculous, completely ridiculous. Why only a total fool would—"

"Yeah, sure," said Sayley. "Come off it, *Michael*. Because your name *is* Michael, right? Your name is Michael Amberson and you believe we exist, and I know you believe it, so you might as well just admit it."

"How did you know my name? How could you—" He stared at Sayley, a frightened look on his face. Then his eyes grew wide. "You are!" he said. "You *are* Sayley! The eyes! I can tell by your eyes! And this *is* Coren and Lenora! I knew it! I knew it wasn't just stories! Oh, this is the happiest, most scrumptious day of my life!"

"Sayley," Coren said, bewildered. "What's going on here? I thought you said that nobody in this world could possibly believe that—"

"Never mind, Coren," said Lenora, giving him a meaningful look.

"But Lenora," he said, ignoring the look, "I don't understand why—"

"Just never mind, Coren," she repeated, this time jabbing him in the arm. Lenora had been watching the conversation between Sayley and the boy. She could see that his very presence made Sayley uncomfortable—although not, she also noticed, particularly unhappy. In fact, even as Sayley was shouting angrily at Michael, she was gazing at him as if he were the most wonderful-looking creature she had ever seen. It was clear that making herself into a god was not the only foolish little game Sayley had been playing while making up this place. No, this boy represented something special to her—something *very* special.

And Sayley was obviously very embarrassed about it—probably would be mortified for them even to know that she might have any interest at all in any boy. Lenora gave Coren just one more jab to make sure he got the point.

Remembering her own girlish fantasies about dark-haired knights with white teeth and magnificent muscles, Lenora smiled to herself and gave the boy an appraising glance. So this was Sayley's idea of perfection—a boy almost as thin as Coren but nowhere near as adorable; he didn't have a single freckle. But he had huge, expressive eyes that were, at this very moment, expressing his awe of Sayley, and a very sweet smile. Come to think of it, he looked a little like that Skwoe boy, Mudd—except the ever so earnest Mudd never smiled.

Well, there was no time to think about that now. Coren was standing there, looking totally bewildered and somewhat in pain, while Sayley glared angrily at him, looking like she was about to punch him in the mouth, and Michael gazed adoringly at Sayley.

"I'll explain later, Coren," Lenora mumbled under her breath. "Just shut up."

"Yes," said Sayley firmly. "Do."

"You know," Michael sighed as he spoke to Sayley, "I love the color of your eyes when they glow like that! Sort of an emerald green with glints of pure gold!"

"Oh, for heaven's sake," wailed Sayley. "Stop that right now!" The horrible thing was, she had been thinking almost the same thing about *his* eyes. One look at this boy and she was . . . well, she didn't know *what* the matter with her was. Her knees felt wobbly and her heart was thudding in her chest, and it wasn't just that he was so handsome—although, no question about it, he was the most handsome boy she'd ever seen.

Of course he was, she reminded herself, feeling even more ashamed. He was exactly as she'd imagined him. For once she was glad Coren didn't have his powers and couldn't hear her thoughts.

"Lenora," she sputtered, "let's get out of here right away, before anything else . . . I mean, let's just *do* it."

Coren turned to Michael. "Let me explain, Michael. We came to this place against our will."

"I can see that," said Michael, his gaze still fixed on Sayley. "It certainly isn't anywhere as interesting as Andilla or Grag or Gepeth—I especially like Gepeth! Sayley's country! *Your*—" He gave Sayley a shy but adoring look.

"Anyway," Coren went on, "now that we're here, our powers don't work—which means we can't imagine ourselves home again."

"And the thing is," Sayley interrupted, speaking very quickly, "they don't work because nobody here in Winnipeg believes in them, and so here they aren't real, but you, Michael Amberson, really do believe we are us—don't ask me why, but you do, and that's just the way it is—and you also believe that Andilla and Gepeth aren't just fantasies and that they really exist and so we want you to concentrate and tell yourself that we really are here and we really do have powers, and then with any luck at all we will have them and we'll be able to imagine ourselves out of this horrible mess and I swear I will never ever use my powers for anything ever again, cross my heart and hope to die!"

For a moment Michael just stared at her—and Lenora and Coren and Sayley stared hopefully back at him.

"Gosh, Sayley," he finally said. "I don't really have to concentrate. I do believe in you, all the time. I mean, I've been awfully ashamed about it, and I haven't told a single person, but ever since I first read *Of Two Minds*, I somehow just *knew* it was all real. I've even dreamed of going to Gepeth myself someday and meeting Sayley and having an adventure with her all of my own. I once wrote the authors a letter and asked them if anything like that had ever happened to them. I knew they'd say 'No, of course not,' and that's exactly what they did say in the letter they sent me back, along with some stuff about how wonderful the imagination is and how it can take you to places you can't go to in reality. But I couldn't take their word for it, I couldn't. I just *knew*. And you know, I've thought again and again about meeting Sayley and—"

"Nobody wants to hear about any of that," Sayley quickly interrupted.

"Oh," said Michael. "Whatever you say, Sayley. You're the boss." He gave her a huge, admiring smile.

"Yes," said Sayley. "I am. And don't you forget it. Now, Michael, you go ahead and think about how you believe in us, while Lenora and I try to imagine us back home. All right?"

He nodded. "Although," he said, "I really don't have to do anything different from usual."

Sayley and Lenora closed their eyes and they concentrated hard. As hard as they possibly could.

When they opened their eyes, they were still standing in the entrance to the convention hall.

"Nothing," Lenora sighed, gazing around despondently.

"Nothing at all," Sayley repeated. "And he's the only one— he was our absolute only chance! We'll be stuck in this awful place forever. I don't want to be here!"

She really didn't want to be there—not with Michael standing so close. She hated the way it made her feel. Why did it make her feel so good?

## Chapter 18

"I don't understand," said Lenora. "Why didn't it work? I mean, if he really does believe in us—"

"I do," said Michael earnestly. "I really do."

"Perhaps," Coren said, "just one believer isn't enough. I mean, with so many nonbelievers around, maybe his belief isn't strong enough to break through—not on its own."

Lenora turned to Sayley. "Are you *sure* he's the only one?"

"Absolutely," said Sayley. "We're doomed."

For a moment there was only a gloomy silence.

"I know!" Coren said, his face lit with a smile. "The trick is to get some of the others to believe in us too, correct? If they knew that Michael already believes in us, well, maybe they'd start to have doubts about us being fakes, too."

"They'd sure have doubts about my sanity," said Michael. Suddenly his eyes grew wide. "You're . . . you're not thinking of telling them, are you? Oh, please, don't tell me that you're going to tell them!"

Coren gave Michael a guilty look. "I'm sorry," he said, "but it looks like it might be our only chance."

"Oh, no!" said Michael in a panicky voice. "I can't let you— I can't. I mean, not that I have many friends to begin with, but after people knew *that*, well, it'd be terrible. They'd think I was crazy. They'd drag me off to the nuthouse."

"Michael," said Sayley, her voice firm. "Be quiet."

Michael's mouth immediately shut tight.

"Yes, Sayley," he mumbled.

"If Coren thinks it will work," Sayley continued, "then we have to try it. You *are* going to tell people about us, Michael. You are going to do it for me—for Sayley. Right?" She gave him a commanding gaze.

For a moment he couldn't speak, his face a turmoil of different emotions. Then, finally, in a small voice he said, "Yes, Sayley, of course. You know what's best. Whatever you want."

But despite what he said Lenora could tell he was terribly worried. In fact, this whole business distressed her. She could understand Sayley's feeling that nobody ever let her have her own way—she'd felt it often enough herself. But for the little girl to turn around and invent someone who believed totally in her and seemed to worship the ground she walked on, and who simply bowed to her every wish and whim even when it was obviously torturing him to do so—well, it was cruel and thoughtless of Sayley, no question about it. How could she do such a thing?

And yet, Lenora realized, her spirits sinking, it had to be done. It did indeed seem to be their only chance. It was selfish, perhaps, to put her own welfare—and that of Coren and Sayley, too, of course—before Michael's feelings. But what else could they do?

And if it worked, well, no one would think Michael was

strange anymore, would they? So really, he had nothing to worry about.

Unless, of course, it didn't work. In which case, Lenora supposed, she and Coren and even the Divine Sayley herself would be joining Michael in the nuthouse.

"Now," said Sayley in a crisp voice, "let's get down to business. What we need is a lot of people for Michael to tell about us—the more the merrier."

Michael's face grew even more pained, if that was possible.

"Where," Sayley continued, looking around, "can we find lots of people? Everyone seems to have cleared out of this place. I can't remember where I've made them all go. Michael? Any ideas?"

His voice was very small. "Do I have to tell you?"

"Yes," said Sayley briskly. "You do."

"It's four o'clock," he said reluctantly, "time for the closing ceremonies of the convention. Everyone must have gone there."

"Yes, of course," said Sayley. "Perfect. Where is it again?"

"In the big hall," Michael said, his voice a bare whisper. "Up the escalators."

"Oh, good," said Sayley cheerfully. "Escalators was one of my best ideas—and now I get a chance to try them out. Let's go."

After a disappointingly boring ride—Sayley concluded that her original idea of blowing people between floors on strong jets of air had been better than escalators after all—they found themselves in a large, barnlike room that was filled with people, most of them dressed up as Lenora and Coren.

They had just settled themselves in the front row, near the door, when a young girl got up on stage and asked everyone to pray for Sayley to come into their lives and be with them. As people bent their heads and began to pray Lenora could sense

Sayley, sitting beside her, becoming more and more restless. Then, before Lenora or Coren could stop her, Sayley leaped from her seat, ran up to the stage, and climbed the stairs to stand beside the girl.

"I've arrived!" she exclaimed. "I'm right here! Your prayers are answered!"

There was a silence throughout the theater. Then, after a moment or two, nervous laughter.

Sayley gave them a look of annoyance. "It is me, you know! Really. Oh, I know you find it hard to believe—if anyone should know it, it's me, because I made you that way. But it's true, and I have someone here who can tell you it's true. Michael! Michael Amberson? Come on up here!"

His face scarlet, Michael rose from his seat and slowly began to make his way forward, his eyes fixed firmly on the floor.

"Not tomorrow, Michael," said Sayley impatiently. "Now!"

"Yes, Sayley!" said Michael, and he quickly ran up on the stage, where he stood beside Sayley, looking like a lamb about to be slaughtered.

"She's certainly as pushy as the Sayley in the book," somebody called out from the audience. Everyone laughed.

Sayley glared out from the stage, hands planted firmly on her hips. "Just who do you think you are calling pushy?" she said. Everyone laughed again.

"Talk about gratitude," said Sayley. "But you'll soon change your tune. Tell them, Michael—go ahead and tell them."

"I've spoken to her," he said, his voice barely audible. "I believe her."

"What?" a number of people shouted. "I can't hear him." They had all turned and were talking to one another, trying to figure out what he had said.

"Louder, Michael," said Sayley.

"I BELIEVE HER!" Michael shouted. A hush fell on the theater as the crowd, dead silent now, stared at him. "This is Sayley!" he continued, not quite so loudly. "The real one. She's not just a character in a book. I'm not crazy. Really. I'm not."

Coren grabbed Lenora's hand. "Lenora, this could be it. If they all believe her, then there's bound to be enough energy here to let you wish us home." Coren looked around the theater. Was there *any* hope that these people would believe her?

"She does look sort of like the Sayley in the books," someone shouted out.

"No way," someone else called. "The Sayley in the books is scrumptiously beautiful."

There was a murmur of assent. Sayley's face darkened dangerously.

"And anyway," another voice added, "the Sayley in the books isn't the Divine Sayley!"

"Of course not!" said a number of others.

"That's sacrilege!"

"It's just plain sick."

"Of course it is," shouted Michael over the voices from the crowd. "I'm not saying she's the Divine Sayley, the creator of us all! I'm not that crazy!"

"Although to tell the truth," Sayley began, "I did actually—"

"Sayley, no!" shouted Lenora. It was going to be hard enough for them to believe a character in a fantasy book was real. And if they ever found out that Sayley had actually made their miserable world and put them in it, well, who could blame them for any amount of damage they might do to her?

"But," Michael said into the silence created by Lenora's interruption, "she *is* the Sayley from *More Minds*. She is, really!"

"Yeah, sure! And just how do you know that, buddy?"

"Yeah," a number of voices called out. "How?"

"It's . . ." Michael hesitated, looking very confused. "It's just a feeling," he said finally. "I just *know* it."

"You're both nuts!" someone called out.

"Yeah," another voice jeered. "You oughta both be in the nut-house!"

A number of people laughed.

"If you're really Sayley," a loud voice suddenly called out, "then why don't you prove it?"

"Yeah," others chimed in. "Prove it! Prove it! Prove it!" Soon the whole hall was screaming in unison.

"QUIET!" It was the girl who had been leading the prayer. Her very loud shout immediately silenced everybody else. "Let's have some order." Then she turned to Sayley. "They're right, you know, dear. I mean, if you're Sayley, you can use your Gepethian powers to create anything, correct?"

"Correct," agreed Sayley. "But—"

"So, then," a loud voice called out from the audience. "Create something! Make something appear! Prove it!"

The crowd began chanting again. "Prove it! Prove it! Prove it!"

The girl gestured them to quiet down again. Soon they all sat in an expectant hush, waiting to see what Sayley would do next.

"Well," Sayley said slowly into the silence, "the thing is, my powers don't work while I'm here. It's because—" The loud jeering began even before she had finished.

"Of course she can't do it!" someone yelled. "She's a fake!"

"Fake! Fake!" others shouted

"Get off the stage, loser!" someone added.

Coren pulled at Lenora's hand. "Lenora, this is getting ugly. We have to help her." They leaped up and ran onto the stage as the crowd laughed and shouted.

"Sayley," Coren whispered, "tell them that if they will just believe in you for *one* minute, you will disappear and *then* you'll create all sorts of new things for them. And," he added, "as soon as they do that, you and Lenora *must* imagine us out of here."

Sayley nodded.

"I *am* Sayley," she said. "You must believe me. Believe in me and you'll see what I can do!"

"Yeah, right!"

"As if!"

"Get a life!"

"*I* believe her," Michael shouted—and this time Sayley hadn't even asked him. He looked really angry now. "What I *can't* believe is how ignorant you people all are! Don't you have eyes? She *is* Sayley. It's perfectly obvious, and I don't care if I do end up in the nuthouse for saying it. She is!"

He stood staring defiantly out at the audience, daring them to tell him he was wrong. Well, Lenora thought, she had to hand it to Sayley. She'd done an excellent job with Michael, truly excellent. And if he was Sayley's idea of the kind of boy she'd like to have adore her, then Sayley certainly had good taste, for a ten-year-old. Almost as good as Lenora's own. She took Coren's hand and gave it an affectionate squeeze.

"And what's more," Michael added, "these are Coren and Lenora here! The real ones!"

"That's not Lenora," someone called. "Lenora isn't *real*!"

"They're just *characters*," another voice added. "Get a grip."

"No. We *are* real," Sayley pleaded. "We are! We just need you to believe us."

"Why would Gepethians need our help?" a young man called. "That makes no sense."

A hush fell on the crowd again. Everyone thought about that.

And suddenly someone yelled, "Get off the stage!"

"Phoney," screamed another voice.

"Fake!"

"Get out of here!"

Soon the entire hall was shouting, and the shouting got worse and worse until Michael grabbed Sayley's hand. "We have to leave. They'll turn on you, and it could get really ugly."

"Oh, I'd like to turn them all into cabbages," Lenora muttered. "Or . . . or slimy slugs living underneath cabbages!"

Coren pushed her and Sayley ahead of him. "Michael's right," he said. "Let's get out of here!"

"Fakes! Phonies!"

"Call for security!"

As the four of them rushed through the door they could hear an angry chorus of calls for Security filling the room behind them.

## Chapter 19

"This is good," said Lenora through a mouthful of food. "What did you call it? A doughnut?"

"Yes," said Michael, his mouth also stuffed. "Honey glazed."

"This peculiar fizzy drink is good, too," said Lenora, smacking her lips. She turned to Sayley and whispered to her, hoping Michael wouldn't hear her and realize the part Sayley had played in his existence, "This world isn't completely horrible, Sayley. At least you put some sensible food in it."

"I did think of making it only vegetables," Sayley whispered back. "Nothing to eat but cabbage and the occasional turnip. But that seemed *too* terrible. See, I didn't want it to be completely—" She suddenly stopped, her face reddening.

*Aha,* thought Lenora, helping herself to another doughnut from the bag on the table in front of her. *Sayley is thinking about Michael now. He's sort of like these doughnuts—she couldn't resist thinking up something wonderful and then putting him in here even if he wasn't horrible at all.* Quite the contrary, if the look on

Sayley's face whenever she got up the courage to actually take a furtive glance at Michael meant anything. From the way she gazed at him, he might as well have been honey glazed also.

The four of them were sitting in a brightly lit room full of tables near the top of the moving stairway in Portage Place. Michael called it a coffee shop. It had become embarrassingly clear to them that, what with just about everybody in the entire place calling for Security whenever they caught sight of them, the convention place was not exactly the best spot for them to be. So Michael had led them through the corridors back to what Sayley called the shopping mall, giving Sayley his coat and freezing as they all crossed the short open spaces full of still-falling snow outside. With any luck, the Security in the mall—this place did seem to have more than its share of Security—would have forgotten about them by now. After Coren had suggested they find somewhere quiet to warm up and reconnoiter so they could figure out their next step, Michael had brought them to the coffee shop. And when he learned that they had no money, he had offered to pay for their food and drinks without Sayley even having to suggest it to him.

Michael was a true gentleman—just like Coren. *No question about it*, Lenora told herself as she took a sip of her drink and enjoyed the interesting tickling sensation of the bubbles bursting against her nose, *he is a prince among boys*. He had Coren's good mind, too. It was easy to see where Sayley had got some of her ideas for him—not just from Mudd. Yes, Sayley definitely had excellent taste.

"It was foolish of me to assume that one person would make a difference," said Coren ruefully. "I mean, really, everyone else suddenly starting to have doubts because one person contradicts what the rest of them all agree with? It's like something in some silly fantasy novel. I thought that all I had to do was wish it and it would come true. That had about as much chance of happening as . . . as pigs flying!"

"But Coren," said Lenora. "Didn't you study any geography at all when you were young? Pigs *can* fly—in Airbornia. Everything flies there—the people, the houses, even the pigs."

"So it was a bad example," said Coren gloomily. "The thing is, we're here now in this awful place and we're stuck here. Probably forever."

"It not like you to give up, Coren," said Lenora, alarmed. "I do hope this lack of imagination isn't catching. Oh, I hate this place! I just hate it!"

"It's not really all that bad," said Michael. "You do like the doughnuts, don't you? And it only snows eight months out of the year, and we have beautiful summers." For a moment he looked perplexed. "That is, I think we do. It really is odd, isn't it? I mean, in one way I feel like I've lived here forever—all my life. But when I try to remember anything specific before yesterday . . . well, I can't. It's like my memory only goes back a couple of days. Is that . . . well, is it normal?"

It wasn't fair to leave Michael so confused, Lenora told herself. It was time he knew the truth. "Actually," she said, "I think I can explain that."

"Do you have to?" said Sayley, squirming.

"He's going to have to know sooner or later, Sayley. And the sooner the better."

"I suppose so," said Sayley. "Blast."

As Sayley bent down and carefully studied the remains of the doughnuts on the table, Lenora went on to tell Michael how and why Sayley had made his world.

After she finished, Michael sat silent for a moment, looking very upset. "So . . . you mean," he said slowly, looking at Sayley, "this was the worst place you could think of?"

Sayley, completely mortified, nodded.

"And," he said, "you put us all here? My parents? My brothers? Me? *You* created me, and you put me and my family into the worst possible place of all?"

Sayley nodded again. "But," she said in an urgent voice, "I made it so no one here would know that. I mean, *you* didn't know it yourself, right, until Lenora opened her big mouth and told you. Why, you were just saying how it wasn't so bad, how you liked it."

"I do. I do like it. It's just that—"

"Of course you like it," Sayley interrupted. "I'm not cruel, you know."

"But," Michael continued, "if *you* think it's horrible, and if you put me in here—and even, I suppose, made me think it was okay, even when you thought it was anything but—well, I should hate you! But"—he paused, completely confused—"I can't. Somehow, I want to forgive you. Why is that?"

"Well, you see, Michael," Coren began, "she—"

"Just never you mind, Coren," Sayley spat out.

"No, Coren don't!" said Lenora at the same time.

For a moment Coren looked at the two of them. Then he shook his head back and forth. "I give up," he said, and he slumped back into his gloomy depression.

"So I guess I was wrong," Michael said. "I guess you really are Sayley our creator, not just the Sayley in the books. It's hard to believe—I've never been a very religious person, I'm more the spiritual type. But I guess I have to believe it now."

Sayley, looking very embarrassed, nodded.

"But," Michael added, "how come I'm the only one here who ever actually believed you're real? You have no idea how many sleepless nights I've spent—and come to think of it, *I* have no idea either. But there I was, tossing in my bed, worrying about whether or not I'm crazy, worrying about what would happen if anybody found out. Which they now have, which means I can probably never show my face in public ever again. What's *that* all about?"

This, Sayley told herself, was even more embarrassing than she could ever have possibly imagined in her wildest dreams. How could she tell Michael that she'd put him in here because she was so proud of this totally awful world she had created, and couldn't bear the thought of nobody in it really believing that she, their clever creator, existed, even though the whole point of it was that nobody in it was supposed to really believe anything? She had told herself that one little exception would be totally harmless—and if she was making an exception, it might as well be not only someone who absolutely appreciated and adored her, but also someone who was exactly the kind of person she would have most liked to have appreciate and adore her. Oh, she couldn't! She couldn't tell him any of that, ever. He'd hate her for it—and that was the very last thing she wanted. Just look at his lovely eyes!

"If we ever do get back home," said Lenora to Michael, "I can promise you that things will be different. Won't they, Sayley?"

"Yes," said Sayley. "They will. I promise. I'll fix everything. I'll make *everyone* believe we exist."

"Let's not be too hasty, Sayley," said Lenora. "From what I've seen here, it seems that the lack of imagination is the key to everything—except, maybe, the doughnuts. If you changed that . . . well, it wouldn't be the same place at all. Everyone would become confused and disoriented."

"Well, then," Sayley said hopefully, "maybe Michael could come back with us to Andilla. Since he really doesn't belong here—"

"I'd love to see Andilla," said Michael. "And all the other places in the books. Especially Gepeth—I'd love to see the countryside of Gepeth! Sayley's home!"

"And," said Coren bitterly, briefly looking up toward them, "just how is he going to do that? When *we* can't even get out of here."

"There has to be some way out," said Lenora. "There *has* to. Maybe we should go back to that store place where the edge was—remember, Coren, where Sayley saw us? We could stand there and try to catch someone's attention—like my parents or yours, Coren. There's bound to be a lot of people up there in the Meeting of Minds exhibit now that the judging is taking place. Once they know we're here, all the Gepethians can get together and easily think us out."

"What did you say?" Michael asked, excited.

"I said, all the Gepethians can—"

"No, no, about the exhibit. You mean we are actually in some kind of small display? I'm actually much smaller than you guys normally are?"

Lenora nodded, expecting Michael to be disoriented by this information or, more likely, angered by it. Being told you were imagined into existence by a girl younger than yourself was bad enough—how would he react to knowing she'd made him as a miniature, like a doll or toy?

Michael was too excited to consider the significance of what he'd just heard. "That means we're in Andilla already! We don't have to get back there because we *are* there!"

"I suppose so," said Lenora, mystified by his excitement.

"But we're still trapped in here," said Coren bleakly, "so it doesn't make any difference. And anyway, how can we go back to that place with the wall considering all those Security—"

"But it *does* make a difference!" said Michael. "A big

difference. I mean, I thought your world was in, like, some kind of parallel universe or something—a place you could get into only if you had magical powers, like you guys usually do. But if we're there already—well, then all we have to do is find some way out past those walls you were talking about—a hole or something. That's much easier—it's just a question of finding a way out!" He turned to Sayley. "There has to be one somewhere, right?"

Coren, Lenora, and Sayley stared at Michael. Then they stared at one another. Then Lenora began to laugh. And soon Sayley joined her.

Coren's face, on the other hand, turned bright red. He was embarrassed. Why hadn't it occurred to him? It was so obvious. They *were* in Andilla, after all. And there had to be holes in the exhibit—otherwise, how would the creatures in it be able to breathe? No question about it, he had been thinking all wrong. Finding himself in a different world, he'd started to believe in it as if it *were* real. But it was only a display, in the ballroom, in *his* castle, in Andilla.

"Sayley," Lenora asked breathlessly as her laughter finally subsided. "Is Michael right? Are there holes?"

"Not holes, exactly," said Sayley. "I didn't want anybody to fall out accidentally and hurt themselves. But there are openings. At the top."

"The top?"

"Yes, where the sky would be. I left spots up there open so air could get in but people wouldn't be likely to fall out. The openings are way up high over their heads."

"Our heads, too, right?" said Coren, his spirits sinking. "Which means they won't be easy for us to get at either."

"Sure they will," said Michael. "All we need is the right equipment. And I know just where to get it. There's a sports store on the other side of the mall, and I bet they'll have what we need—indoor rock climbing equipment."

"Indoor rock climbing?" Lenora turned to Sayley. "What kind of strange idea is that?"

"It's only logical, Lenora," said Sayley. "Everyone does everything inside here. I mean, it's so cold outside, right? Who would want to go rock climbing out in all that wind and snow? Besides which, I made the land all around this place perfectly flat—just so it'd be really plain and boring, you know? I even *called* it the plains. There are no mountains to climb, not even any little hills. But of course the people love the idea of rock climbing, just because it's so completely impossible for them—that's just another part of the horribleness, always wanting what you can't have. So they make do with fake rock walls indoors."

"Yes," said Michael. "It's a very popular activity here. That, tanning studios, and scuba diving in indoor pools are the most popular ones. Oh, and hockey, too, of course. But gosh, are there really actual mountains somewhere, I mean, actually outside, that you can climb? I always sort of thought there were! Amazing!"

Coren was not quite ready to give up his doubts. "But we'd have to find a hole near a climbable wall, right, so even if we do get the equipment—"

"Oh, Coren," said Lenora impatiently, "don't be so negative. There's bound to be some opening close to a wall we can climb. Right Sayley?"

"I . . . I suppose so. It's hard to remember all the details—and it looks so different when you're inside."

"So," Lenora continued, "all we have to do is find the right place. Let's get busy. Coren, you go with Michael to get this climbing equipment, and meanwhile, Sayley and I will see if we can find a good spot for us to climb out."

"I suppose," Coren sighed, "we'll have to steal the equipment. Oh well, what difference will yet a few more Security men chasing after us make? The more the merrier."

"Don't worry about it," Michael said. "We won't have to steal anything. I have the money in my account. We just have to stop off at a machine and get it. I work for my neighbors, see, shoveling their walkways. You can make a *lot* of money that way here. A *lot*."

Lenora nodded. "Excellent. You two go get the equipment, and Sayley and I will go up to the top floor and see if we can find a good spot to try. We'll meet you up there at the top of the moving stairway." She paused and gave Michael a radiant smile. "Are you going to come with us, Michael? To Andilla, I mean?"

"I'd really like to see your worlds," said Michael, "I really truly would. But my mother and father and my sister would be awfully upset if I just sort of disappeared. And I'd miss them, too. Especially my mom. If I could come for a visit maybe— not now, of course, because I'd have to ask my folks for permission first and bring along my toothbrush and a change of underwear. But someday, perhaps . . ." He got a dreamy look in his eyes. It was as if no matter how truly he believed in the existence of Andilla and Gepeth, he couldn't really imagine himself being there—as if that were quite beyond possibility. He was a citizen of the world Sayley had created, after all.

And for him, thought Lenora, that world was real. Real people lived in it, and he had real feelings about them. No question about it, having imaginative powers like Sayley and herself was a serious responsibility.

"If we get back," Coren said, smiling at Michael, "Lenora or Sayley can always bring you to Andilla."

"Of course," said Sayley. She tried to hide her disappointment.

Why couldn't he just come with them now? He was so adorable!

"First we have to see if we can do this," Lenora said. "Come on, Sayley. We have work to do."

# Chapter 20

"Sayley and I think that the easiest access is right over there." The four of them were standing just at the top of the escalator, beside a large, shiny bag containing the equipment Michael and Coren had purchased, facing into the courtyard that spread beneath them and all around them. Lenora was pointing over their heads, to a place on the left of the skylight, close to where it met a wall.

"I remember putting an airhole there," said Sayley. "You can't see it from here, because I made it look like the rest of the skylight from the inside."

His hand shielding his eyes, Coren looked to where they were pointing. The wall it was close to stretched the whole length of the space they stood in and had only one opening, a large doorway near one end with a brightly lit sign over it that said RIALTO BIJALTO. Except for a few small pictures hung at eye level, it was just a bare wall of pink and turquoise bricks all the way up to where it met the skylight.

"If we do go up there and then go over that wall," said Coren, gazing at where she was pointing, "won't we fall into whatever place is on the other side of the wall? Rialto Bijalto?"

"No," said Sayley, "because there isn't anything on the other side. I couldn't decide what that Rialto Bijalto place should be—either a big room where people go and lose all their money betting on racing horses and things, or else a food place where they serve nothing but the eyes of different kinds of animals. Since I couldn't decide, I just made that wall an edge."

"Which," Lenora said, "makes it the perfect place for us. We can climb down the other side into Andilla, and imagine ourselves back to the right size again, and go get Leni."

"Sounds perfect," Coren said. "The only problem is that it's going to be almost impossible to get up there." The impediment, he could see, was a ledge that stuck out from the wall. It protruded so far out that if they used their equipment to climb up the wall, they'd have real trouble making their way over it.

"No, it isn't," said Lenora. "We can just go that way." She pointed at the clock in the middle of the courtyard. The huge face loomed directly in front of them.

Coren gasped. It was true that the clock had a nice flat roof—and that from there it would be an easy matter of swinging a rope with a hook up into the girders supporting the skylight and then making their way to the right spot. But though the clock was clearly visible from where they stood, one of its four large faces directly in front of them, the clock tower itself stood on the ground floor of the courtyard, its base extending two levels below. Between them and it was a large expanse of nothing but empty space, open air. Air all the way down to the very hard floor below. Air they would have to cross to get to the clock. The mere thought of it was enough to make Coren's stomach lurch.

"Lenora," he said, "you can't be serious."

"I am absolutely serious. We just get a rope attached up there, at the top of the clock, then we tie the other end here on this railing and simply scoot right on over there."

Was she mad? Couldn't they just go down to the main floor and climb up the clock tower from there? No—they didn't have the time. But still—

"It's too exposed," Coren said. "I mean, sure, there aren't many people up on this level, but as soon as the people down below see us dangling out there in the middle of nowhere on a rope—"

"We could *scare* them away," Sayley suggested. "We'll make faces and scream, and they'll get scared and run away."

"And call Security," Coren said.

"Oh," said Sayley. "Right. I am very sorry about security. It was *not* a good idea."

"We could set off the fire alarm," Michael suggested.

"Fire alarm?" said Coren.

"It's a very loud noise," Sayley explained, "and when it goes off, everyone has to get out of the building. I made it really undependable, so that it would go off all the time and everyone would have to go out and stand in the snow two or three times a day."

"That was mean, Sayley," Lenora commented.

Michael nodded. "Very mean," he agreed. "I hate false alarms, especially when you don't have time to get your coat. But right now they're very handy for us. See, you three could go hide in the bathrooms—they're just over there"—he pointed in the other direction from the bare wall—"inside the Plains Theater Center. There's no play on now, so you won't have a problem getting inside there without tickets. I'll give you enough time to get in, and then I'll set off the alarms. Security will check everywhere to make sure the whole place is empty, so don't let them see you. And then once security is gone, you can come out here and set up your equipment. You won't have long before they realize it's a false alarm, but at least it'll give you a start."

"Excellent as usual, Michael," Lenora said. "Let's do it!"

There seemed to be no choice. Sighing, and trying not to think about what was between himself and the clock, Coren picked up the heavy bag, and the three of them headed for the bathrooms. They all slipped through the door that said WOMEN—Coren fervently hoping there was no one else in there already—went into the toilet stalls, and stood on the toilets so no one could see they were there.

Within minutes they heard a horrible ringing so loud it made Lenora grit her teeth. Sure enough, a short time later the door opened and someone looked in. They held their breath as a man's voice called out, "Anyone in here?" When he received no answer, he left. They breathed again, then waited another couple of minutes and hurried back to the railing on the walkway between the top escalators, hoping Security was no longer close enough to see them.

"What do we do with that?" asked Lenora, gazing in perplexity at the equipment Coren was pulling from the bag and laying out on the floor.

"The person in the store explained how it worked," Coren said. He picked up a metal hook attached to a rope. "First, we throw this out and try to get it caught up there." Nervously swallowing, he glanced over at the top of the clock. It seemed so near, so tantalizingly near—and yet so dangerously far. "With a good strong throw we should be able to get it hooked there—and hope it holds."

"And then," Lenora said enthusiastically, "we just climb over the railing and go hand over hand! And once we're at the top of the clock, it'll be really easy to throw the rope again and get the hook up over that girder. We'll be where we want to be in no time. Excellent!"

Coren looked unhappily at the hook, and then once more at the clock. "It doesn't really look very safe to me."

"Oh, Coren," Lenora chided him. "Michael said that people use these things all the time. It must be safe—and it sounds like fun. Once we're up there, though, how do we get down on the other side?"

"Couldn't we just imagine ourselves down?" said Sayley.

"I don't think so," said Lenora. "I suspect that nothing is going to work until we have no contact with this place at all— not even standing on top of it. I suppose, though, that once we're up there we could jump off and imagine ourselves bigger before we land—oh, and Coren, too, of course. We'll have to imagine him bigger, too."

"No," said Coren firmly. Lenora sounded so excited by the idea of jumping that if she did do it, she'd probably forget about him altogether, and there he'd be on the floor in Andilla, tiny and squashed and about to be walked on by some of the wedding guests. Suddenly the equipment was looking much safer to him. "We'll use this stuff," he said. "The first one up also carries these extra ropes. This other one with a hook can go over the girder, and the third one, well, it should be long enough to reach all the way down to the bottom. Whoever goes first will have to tie that rope around the girder, throw it out the hole, and then slowly drop down the other side."

"It sounds like the first person has all the fun," said Lenora. "Can I do it?"

Trust Lenora to think that putting herself in the position of falling from a great height would be fun. "Be my guest," said

Coren. "And then Sayley, and then me last." Although, he thought, being the last person left, dangling in midair without anyone else around to call to for help if help was needed, would be almost as dangerous as being the first up.

As Coren helped Lenora organize all the equipment she needed, and helped her to loop the ropes around her neck, Michael came puffing up the escalator.

"I was hiding downstairs," he said, panting. "I had to wait until the security men went outside. Are you ready? Because they'll all start coming back in any minute now."

Coren nodded. "Ready as we'll ever be," he said.

"You've been a great help, Michael," said Lenora. "I hope we meet again." She looked up. "Stand back while I throw this hook."

It took a couple of tries, but she soon had the hook lodged over the top edge of the clock. Coren took the other end of the rope from Lenora, pulled it taut, and tied it on to the railing, making a series of knots. Then he gave it a hard tug to see if it would hold. It seemed to. Which meant they would actually have to go through with this foolhardy business.

In fact, they already were going through with it. With a sudden leap and a whoop of excitement Lenora made her way over the railing, grabbed on to the rope, and hung in midair.

Coren watched anxiously as Lenora swayed precariously, hand moving over hand as she made her way toward the clock. Each time she took off a hand in order to move and dangled from just the one hand left on the rope, his breath caught in his throat and his heart seemed to miss a beat. It was bad enough watching Lenora—would he actually have the nerve to do this himself?

"There," Lenora called out after what seemed like an eternity, lifting herself up onto the top of the clock. "That ought to do it. You can start now, Sayley." Lenora turned and swung the second rope up toward the girder.

Coren could not possibly watch her any longer. He turned to Sayley. "Can you manage?"

"Of course I can," Sayley scoffed. "It'll be easy as pie!" She turned to Michael. "Good-bye," she said shyly, and because she was so embarrassed she practically leaped over the railing onto the rope and had pulled herself halfway across the open space before he could respond.

"Hurry," Michael called, his voice anxious. "The fire trucks are here already!" The loud wail of a siren could be heard from outside.

Now it was Coren's turn. He was terrified. But at least he'd be so busy dangling dangerously in midair, about to fall to a certain death, that he wouldn't have to watch Lenora and Sayley make their way up the even higher rope that now hung down from the girder over the clock.

"What's going on here?"

Coren turned to see two children staring up at Sayley, who was standing on the roof of the clock watching Lenora make her way up the second rope. Two familiar-looking children. It was the two girls who had stolen the toy bear from the smaller girl some hours earlier.

"Hurry up!" Michael urged Coren. "I'll deal with these kids."

So Coren pulled himself over the railing, grabbed the rope, and began to swing along it. Before he even realized what he was doing, he was quite some distance away from the railing. *Don't look down*, he told himself. *Whatever you do, don't look down.*

Meanwhile, Michael was speaking to the little girls. "It's a tournament," he said. "A climbing tournament."

"Hey," one girl said as she watched Coren, who had reached

the end of the rope and had pulled himself onto the top of the clock, accidentally kicking one of its hands and pushing it downward in the process. "I know him! He's the guy who picked on us before, Abbey!"

"You're right, Minnie," said the other. "It is! Let's call security!"

The first girl nodded, a wicked smile on her face. "SECURITY!" she called. "HELP!" And the second one soon joined in. "HELP! SECURITY!"

As they shouted, the clock began to make a loud sound. Apparently Coren had kicked its hand far enough down to reach the quarter hour. He could feel the chime reverberate right through him, so loudly he nearly let go off the rope. But only nearly.

"I'd better get out of here," Michael shouted to Coren over the girls' loud cries. "Right now! Good luck!"

Coren scrambled away from the edge of the clock and then turned to see Michael already rushing down the moving stairway.

"Stop!" another voice cried out to him. "Stop in the name of the Mall Police!" It was another Security, rushing up the other stairway.

"Here!" the girl named Minnie shouted. "It's a bad guy! Up there on the clock!"

With a gulp Coren grabbed the second rope and began to move upward as quickly as he could. The coast was clear, thank goodness, because Sayley had already made it to the top and had disappeared from view.

"If you don't come down this instant," this Security called up to him, "I'm coming up there after you." Looking down, Coren could see Security still standing by the escalator, nowhere near where the rope was tied to the railing. It was probably just an idle threat—the fellow, more sensible than some people Coren could name, didn't seem to be in any rush to launch himself into midair on a very fragile-looking rope. Nevertheless Coren desperately scurried up the last few feet to the girder and pulled himself up onto it. Then, as fast as he could, he reeled in the rope he'd just been climbing—if this Security ever did take leave of his senses and make his way over to the top of the clock, he wouldn't find it easy to pursue them any farther.

"You'll have to come down sooner or later, buddy," Security shouted, waving his fist at Coren menacingly. "And when you do, I'll be waiting."

Security was right, Coren told himself. He did have to go down sooner or later—but not the way he came. With any luck, Security was going to have a long wait.

Coren turned away from the man and looked around, over the top of the skylight. He was standing on the edge of what looked like vast acres of rooftops, as if he were in the center of a gigantic city. But in fact, he realized, the rooftops were the tops of all the different exhibits in the Meeting of Minds contest. And he'd better make his way down to the table beneath them right away, before Lenora took it into her head to imagine him back to life size and he suddenly grew and squashed flat the entire world of Winnipeg and everyone in it. None of them deserved an awful fate like that—not even Security. Not even those incredibly annoying authors with their weak imaginations and their mysterious underwear.

Sighing, Coren grabbed onto the rope Lenora had hung there and began to make his way down it.

## Chapter 21

Coren slithered down the rope, trying not to let it burn his hands. He glanced around but could see only the wall in front of him—it was surprisingly dark now. And he could feel a breeze. A strong breeze.

He called out. "Lenora? Lenora are you there?"

He was afraid to look down. He didn't want to get dizzy. He kept slithering and sliding as the wind got stronger and stronger. It seemed to be pulling him down. Despite his fear, he knew he had to look down to see what was below—and as soon as he did, his head began to spin. Still, he could make out what seemed to be some kind of alley—a channel with walls on both sides curving off into the distance in the murk below. Shouldn't he be dropping onto the table the displays had been placed upon?

It wasn't an alley down there exactly, more like a . . . a . . . No time left to think about it, because the wind was taking over his mind, occupying all his thoughts. It was getting stronger and stronger, tugging at him, dragging him down. He had to let go of the rope or have his hands torn off. He let go.

He fell at an incredible speed as the wind sucked him down. This wasn't what they had planned. Had Sayley surrounded her city with some nasty wind device and forgotten to mention it?

"Help!" Coren yelled. But the wind took the sound and made it into nothing. He was falling, falling, falling. It was pitch black and he was sliding faster and faster and—

He hit bottom and slammed into something surprisingly soft.

"Oof!" a voice said. "Get off me!"

It was Lenora. He could tell from her voice—and that was the only way he could tell, because it was pitch black, so black he couldn't see the rope dangling in front of his face. He moved his hands, feeling beneath him.

"Coren, stop that! And get *off* me." It was Lenora all right.

Coren almost didn't want to move. He wanted to cling to Lenora. He hated dark places. He hated not knowing where he was. Reluctantly, he rolled away from Lenora and bumped into something else.

"Ouch," said Sayley's voice. "Coren! Honestly!"

"Where are we?" Coren demanded.

"*I* certainly don't know," Lenora remarked. "We should be on the table. Sayley, please *try* to remember. Is this part of your vision?"

"Honestly, Lenora, I'm *sure* it isn't!" Her voice changed, grew alarmed. "Oh! Oh, no!"

"What?"

"I think I know where we are," she said—and by the sound of her voice Coren really didn't think he was going to like what he was about to hear.

"I remember the exhibit beside mine," Sayley continued. "It

came in sixth or seventh. I mean, it wasn't very imaginative. But it was done by quite a young child—eight years old, I think—so the judges felt it should get an honorable mention. And it did have a kind of basic creepy awfulness about it that no one could deny."

"And," Coren said acidly, "just what would that creepy awfulness be?"

"Well, the entire structure is an elaborate maze with no light, no light at all. And there are wind tunnels at both exits, so once you're inside, it's virtually impossible to get out."

"Lovely," Coren said.

"Charming," Lenora added.

"Um, that's not *quite* all," Sayley said reluctantly.

"Go on," said Coren.

She did. "You see, the mazes are filled with the most horrible monsters the little girl could imagine. And I must say, she imagined some really dreadful ones. She put in a small one-way viewing screen on the top, so people could look at them. The monsters can't see out, but people *can* see in."

"What kind of monsters?" Coren asked, his voice beginning to quiver.

"Oh! Every kind! Slimy ones with long tentacles, and big ones with sharp teeth, and smelly ones that could kill you with a whiff, and long prickly ones that can crush you by wrapping themselves around you. All kinds!" Then she paused. And then she started to cry. "We're going to die in here!"

"We are, Lenora," Coren agreed, his hands beginning to tremble.

"Nonsense," Lenora scolded both of them. "That's exactly what you said about Sayley's exhibit—and we got out of that, didn't we?"

"Yes," said Coren, "but—"

"But nothing," said Lenora. "Monsters are *always* stupid. We'll outsmart them."

"Not these," Sayley wailed. "That's one of the things the judges liked. She gave them brains. They're smart—and they love to kill."

"Oh," said Lenora. For a moment there was only silence. Silence and wind and darkness.

"But at least," Lenora finally said, "we're not totally on our own. I mean, she must have put something in here for them to kill."

"No," Sayley said. "She didn't. She actually just gave them already-killed food to eat, because they were so totally despicable, she told the judges, it would be too mean to put anything in here they could really hurt and maim."

"So then," Coren said slowly, "we'll be the first *real* prey they've had."

"There's got to be some way," said Lenora. "Think, Coren."

"Lenora," Sayley whispered. "I can hear something coming." And sure enough, so could Coren—a sort of panting noise barely audible in the howling wind. He had to think. *Think, Coren,* he told himself, *think! Do it now!*

No, wait a minute—that wasn't him telling himself that. It was Lenora. She was speaking inside his mind. He was overhearing her thoughts.

"Of course!" he suddenly exclaimed. "You and Sayley couldn't use your powers before because we were in a world with no imagination. But this world isn't like that, is it? It's dangerous, but it's *not* based on people who have no imagination. When that girl created it, she didn't put people in it at all."

"Hurry!" Sayley squealed. "Do something! It's getting closer!" *Oh,* she added in her thoughts, *we're all going to die, because that Coren is never going to do anything—he's useless, totally useless!*

"I am not useless, Sayley—because my powers are working! And if mine are, then yours and Lenora's must be too! Just imagine us out of here!" A huge, slimy tentacle wrapped itself around Coren's ankle. "Now! Please! Now!"

**C**hapter 22

**A**ll three of them were squished into a dark place. A dark place still, but with no wind or tentacles. A place filled with what felt like—towels.

Well, at least it wasn't tentacles. "Where are we?" Coren asked.

"We're in a closet," Lenora said. "A linen closet near the exhibit hall in the castle. I imagined us somewhere where Leni couldn't see us and send us right back again."

Coren could hardly breathe. He and Sayley and Lenora were squashed together in an uncomfortable heap. But even squashed and barely breathing, Coren was ecstatic. He was home!

"Good thinking, Lenora," he said. "But nevertheless, it's rather cramped in—"

Suddenly the door flew open and a face peeked in.

"Oh!" It was Lenora's mother, Queen Savet. "Lenora, *there* you are. I've been looking everywhere for you. Honestly,

Lenora, all you talk about these days is wedding dresses and wedding decorations, and there are other things we need to focus on, you know, because it's not as if life suddenly stops for everyone else just because *you're* getting married. I mean, there is the small matter of sheets and towels for all your guests. And keeping this palace clean, of course. Those contestants are simply so careless—why, yesterday, in the ball room, I actually stepped on a thumbtack! It was awful! Not to mention that dreadful display of a world of dust, which keeps leaking all over Milda's new parquet. A world of dust, indeed—what twisted minds some people have! And of course they're all such lofty thinkers with their heads in the clouds all the time that none of them ever think to sweep up after themselves, and—"

Pausing for breath, she finally seemed to take in the fact that the three of them were crammed in a closet. Her eyes narrowed.

"I hope," she finally said in a very suspicious voice, "that the three of you aren't plotting something. Because you know, Lenora, your father and I are worried that you've been cooking something up. All this business of pretending not to care about the exhibits. That's not like you, Lenora, not like you at all. And we really have too many guests for you to start creating *anything*, anything at all. Just what are you up to?"

"Mother!" Lenora said, totally ignoring everything she'd said. "I have never been so glad to see you!"

"That's nice, dear. I'm glad to see you, too. But why all the excitement? After all, Lenora, I spoke to you only a moment ago—if you can call it speaking. The nasty way you criticized my choice of accessories! I mean, really, Lenora, is that any way to talk to your own mother? And what's wrong with Maconitorn-encrusted earrings, I'd like to know. They're a family heirloom, too—they belonged to my Great-Aunt Bolna."

"Mother," said Lenora urgently, gazing past her to see if anyone had noticed them there, "we can't be seen. Come in here and I'll tell you all about it."

"Come into the closet? But there's no room. I'll muss up all those nicely folded towels. And I—"

Lenora grabbed her mother's hand, dragged her into the closet, and pulled the door shut behind her. Now it was even more crammed than before.

"Mother, that wasn't me you were just talking to."

"It wasn't? It certainly looked like you, dear. Whose elbow is that? Please remove it from there immediately."

"Oops, sorry," said Coren, moving his elbow.

"Ouch," said Sayley.

"I know it looked like me," said Lenora, "but Coren and Sayley and I haven't even been here."

"You haven't been—?"

"No—we've been trapped in Sayley's exhibit! And guess who put us there? Leni!"

"Leni? Who's—? Oh, yes, of course. Leni. I told you, Lenora, that you'd be sorry you ever—"

"Yes, Mother, I know, you were right. All too right, because Leni's been masquerading as me! And Cori is pretending to be Coren! We have to do something about them, Mother, because they've somehow taken leave of their senses and they're dangerous, really and truly dangerous. It was horrible being stuck in Sayley's vision. It wasn't Sayley's *best* world Leni sent us to. It was her *worst*. And we were afraid we'd never escape!" Lenora actually threw her arms around her mother in relief.

"Oof," said Coren.

"Ouch," said Sayley.

"My sentiments exactly," said Queen Savet. "There seems to be more elbows in here than people. You know, Lenora dear, *you* aren't behaving much like Lenora either. Actually saying your poor dear mother is right about something. *And* hugging me! Maybe *you're* the imposter!"

"Mother, really! Would *I* ever question your choice of accessories? I hardly even know what an accessory *is*."

"That's true, dear." Queen Savet paused. "Are you positive this isn't one of your little jokes? Because if it is, it's a decidedly claustrophobic one—and very bad for the towels."

"No! Now, you must go get Daddy and bring him here so we can decide what to do about those two."

"You aren't going to stay in here, are you?" her mother said. "Because the towels—"

"We aren't, are we, Lenora?" whined Sayley. "I'm famished. And I'm squashed. I want to go to my room."

"We can't let them see we've escaped," Lenora cautioned. "Leni is fast and mean—much meaner than I ever thought she'd turn out to be. She could do it again. You know, to be on the safe side, I think maybe I should simply disappear her."

"I agree," said Sayley. "Then let's eat."

"Now wait a minute," Coren objected, "you can't just disappear those two. They are *real*, Lenora, and after all, you did create them. They're your responsibility. You can't just—"

"Coren," Lenora said, exasperated, "they would have let us die there! And if Leni discovers we've escaped, well, what do you think she's going to do? Be responsible? Worry about doing the right thing?"

Coren thought. "I suppose she *could* disappear *us*. But," he added, "that doesn't make it right for *us* to do it to them."

"Oh, Coren, you are so . . . so . . ." She paused for a moment. "Blast it, anyway. Life was so much easier before you were around and I could be as thoughtless as I wanted."

Coren could feel himself blush again.

"Mother," Lenora continued, "get Daddy and bring him here, right now. We *have* to figure out what to do."

"Maybe you'd better bring my parents, too," Coren suggested. "Cori is their son, sort of."

"I suppose," Lenora said. "But Coren, you can just contact your parents mind to mind."

"I know," Coren said, "but if I did Cori could easily overhear me. We'd better let your mother bring them here."

"All right, dear," said Queen Savet. "I'll do my best. I'll be back as quickly as possible."

Giving Lenora a quick kiss on the cheek, she bustled out of the closet and closed the door behind her. Then she opened it again.

"Lenora dear," she said, "hand me four towels. The Larpenions insist on showering every hour! Really. But at least they appreciate good linens when they see them. Better make it eight."

Lenora quickly counted out eight towels, handed them to her mother, and pushed the door shut behind her. As soon as the door closed, the closet seemed to expand and the three of them could breathe easily again.

Sayley grinned. "Well, we may as well be comfortable."

"But won't the people outside be able to see that it's bigger?" said Coren.

"Nope," said Sayley triumphantly. "I imagined it big on the inside, but the same size as usual on the outside."

That wasn't even physically possible. Coren shook his head in admiration. The child's powers were truly amazing.

Even as he thought it the closet grew brighter, three comfortable chairs appeared, and Sayley's hand held a giant lemon ice.

"Oh," said Sayley, "that felt soooo good. I hated it when my powers didn't work, just hated it. I'm never going to let it happen ever again!"

She wouldn't, either. And everyone thought Lenora was a handful! Poor Gepeth. Poor Andilla. Poor Coren.

"What a good idea," Lenora said, gazing hungrily at Sayley's ice. She made herself one too, but not before creating an orange sherbet for Coren—his favorite. They all munched happily away for a few moments, enjoying the calm of the closet, just glad to be back.

A cautious knock sounded at the door, and Coren's mother spoke to him, mind to mind. *Coren, are you there, dear?*

*Yes, Mother,* Coren thought. *Come in. Is Father with you?*

*I'm right here,* shouted King Arno into Coren's head. *Don't worry, lad!*

The door opened, and Queen Milda and King Arno peeked in. King Rayden, Lenora's father, and Queen Savet were right behind them.

*Unusual place for the heads of state to meet,* Arno thought as he stepped into the closet.

"Speak aloud, Father and Mother," Coren instructed them. "We can't afford to have Cori overhear us."

"Odd place for a meeting," King Rayden thundered.

"Just what I was thinking," King Arno echoed.

"We're *hiding*, Father," Lenora explained.

"Hiding? That's not like you, Lenora."

"Well, I've just been in a very nasty situation," Lenora explained, "thanks to Leni, who has been pretending to be me."

"But Lenora," King Rayden objected, "you've been behaving so well! No upsetting the guests, no wild schemes! Agneth is just beginning to relax. Do you mean to tell me that's because you haven't *been* here? That it's been someone else all along?"

"Yes, Daddy."

"How disappointing."

"Daddy!"

"Oh! Don't mistake me. Naturally I'm delighted to have my daughter back—I wouldn't change you for anything, Lenora, and you know it." He gave her a fond smile. "But Agneth is such a nuisance when he gets upset—all that annoying fussing and hopping. Still, if it means I have *you*, dear . . ." He smiled, paused, and glanced around the closet. "You know, Arno, I never would have suspected this closet would be so roomy. Excellent planning."

"I suppose," said King Arno.

"As you know, Rayden," said Coren's mother, "we Andillans never have much time to think about mundane things like actual closets—too busy living the life of the mind. Which reminds me—I have my exhibit to complete. There are flying chairs to build, invisible clouds to concoct!"

"And don't forget the baking," said King Arno. "Chocolate-chip cookies for six hundred!"

Queen Milda just ignored him. "A world of wonders awaits me, and time's a-wasting! Tell us, children, what is the problem exactly?"

"It's Cori, Mother," said Coren. "He's pretending to be me. Haven't you *noticed*? At all?"

Queen Milda looked a little embarrassed. "Well, dear, I *have* been very busy. Do you know how hard it is to think up a world in the midst of all this chaos? There are more than three hundred guests here now, constantly thinking, thinking, thinking—it's very difficult to concentrate. So frankly, well, I suppose I haven't really had time for a good talk with you— I simply didn't notice, Coren dear."

"You did ask me why he kept going on and on about a new sword, though, didn't you, Milda?" said Arno.

"Why yes, Arno. Yes, I did. Because normally you don't carry a sword at all—do you, Coren dear?"

"No, Mother," Coren said, trying not to lose his patience. "I don't carry a sword. I never have, have I? But Cori does."

"He does, doesn't he?" mused Arno. "Dear me. You poor children. Savet says you've been in some horrible world that little Sayley created. What you need is a hot bath and some good home baking."

"It was *supposed* to be horrible!" Sayley exclaimed in her own defense. "Honestly!"

"I still think we should disappear them," Lenora stated. "I know, I know—it's extreme. But they're dangerous. Who knows what they might do next!"

"She does have a point," Rayden agreed.

"I really don't think we could agree to such a thing," Milda said. "I mean, they *are* our guests. You don't simply disappear your guests."

"But," insisted Sayley, "they've been bad. They should be punished! We *have* to at least take away their powers, or they'll do something else awful to us, I know they will. How would *you* feel if you were stuck in your own worst nightmare?" She almost started to cry again.

"We *could* take away their powers, I suppose," Savet considered. "That way they'd still exist. And actually, only Leni needs her powers curbed. Cori's can't really hurt anyone."

"Unless he eavesdrops where he shouldn't," Coren commented. "And uses what he hears for the wrong reasons."

The door flew open.

"Or the right ones!" Cori exclaimed, waving a naked sword in their faces. "See, Leni? I knew they were in here! I heard it all! The unconscionable varlets are plotting against us! I'll slit all their despicably evil throats, from traitorous ear to traitorous ear!"

"That would be very messy, Cori darling," said Leni from behind him. "Not at all good for the towels. And quite unnecessary."

The closet suddenly became a jail with iron bars—Leni's work, obviously. Without even realizing she was doing it, Lenora immediately began to imagine it back again.

Nothing happened. "Blast," said Lenora.

"Phooey," said Sayley at the same time.

King Rayden also chimed in. "Good heavens!" he said.

*Oh no,* Lenora thought. *I am not the only one.* Leni had imagined them *all* without their powers.

"You bet she did," said Cori. "Good for you, Leni!"

"I . . . I suppose so," said Leni hesitantly. "That is, I didn't actually mean to do it, because it's no good for the Balance, all this awful imagining. But something came over me and . . . well, it's for a good cause, isn't it? Because now no one in Gepeth will ever have to use their powers again. Including me. Actually, it's all for the best—the only way to keep the Balance preserved. Don't you think so, Cori dear?"

"Whatever you say, my love. You *are* totally committed to their throats remaining unslit? Because it would only take a—"

"Maybe later, Cori. After the wedding"—she gave Lenora a triumphant glance—"after *our* wedding, when all the guests have gone home and there's no one around to see and tell on us. For now, I think, they're safe enough in here."

"You can't do this!" Savet wailed. "We'll be missed, won't we, Rayden? Our courtiers will—"

"I hadn't thought of that," said Leni. "But I suppose it's easily solved. I'll just have to create duplicates of you—puppet duplicates who answer only to me, of course, and do everything I tell them to do without question. If I do that, no one will ever know you're gone. But, oh dear—that means yet more imagining, doesn't it? Once you get started, it just goes on and on. There's a lesson in that, Lenora."

A lesson? Lenora glared at her. What had happened to Leni? Disturbing the Balance, being cruel enough to create slaves to obey her every whim—this behavior was so unlike her.

Also, it was completely infuriating. "How dare you?" said Lenora. "Why, if it weren't for my imagination, you wouldn't even exist!"

"Now, now Lenora," Leni said. "Temper, temper. Let's go, Cori dear—I need to consult with Agneth and Fullbright about *my* wedding. Ta ta, all! Honestly, Cori," she said to him as she turned and flounced away, "they were going to disappear us. Can you imagine? My *own* parents. You can't trust anyone these days."

The closet door shut with a huge crash. They were trapped.

Chapter 23

Somehow a single solitary towel had been left behind when Leni transformed the linen closet into a jail. Queen Savet clutched it.

"Rayden," she said, her voice strained, "I certainly can't believe that you have let that snip of a girl overpower you!"

King Rayden blushed. "But it was so sudden. I didn't expect it." He rounded on Lenora. "Lenora, *you* shouldn't have let her. You're young. You're quick. Why didn't you stop her?"

"She had the element of surprise," Lenora sighed. "Sayley and I together could have easily overpowered her, but we didn't get a chance, did we? And why?" She glared at Coren. "Because we were all so busy being little Goody Two-shoes!"

"But it would have been wrong to disappear them," Coren insisted. "I mean, I'll admit that not doing it has had a few unfortunate consequences, but—"

"A few? Hah!" Lenora said angrily. "*And* they were conse-quences I predicted. Honestly! You can't get all moral when you're fighting an enemy. *They* obviously have no scruples at all."

That made everyone pause for a moment, until Sayley broke the silence. "Are we going to be stuck in here *forever?*"

"Of course not!" Lenora said forcefully. "We're bound to figure a way out. We always do. Don't we, Coren?"

Coren tried to nod reassuringly, but he didn't feel reassured. No one knew where they were. If the duplicates of them that Leni said she was going to make behaved appropriately, no one would ever know.

In fact, the whole thing had Coren stymied. When did Leni become so vicious? He certainly hadn't seen it coming. Although, now that it had happened, it did make a chilling sort of sense. Leni shared almost all of Lenora's personality—including Lenora's iron will and her almost impermeable conviction in the rightness of her own ideas. Once Lenora decided that something needed to be done, there wasn't much that was going to stop her from doing it. Leni, it seemed, was like that too—and she had clearly, and quite uncharacteristically, decided that something needed to be done.

Something awful.

Lenora tried to pace, but she couldn't. This was her worst nightmare, even worse than Sayley's horrible world of Winnipeg, where at least there wasn't anyone going on about towels and the Balance all the time. Locked in jail with her parents, and without the power to do anything about it—what could be worse?

Sure enough, her mother started. "Well, Lenora, we're always so busy we never get a chance to really talk do we? And we really must discuss the wedding ceremony and your travel plans, and your *dress*, because now I realize that I've been discussing all that with Leni and that doesn't count, does it?"

"Mother," Lenora said through gritted teeth, "if we never get out of here, Leni and Cori will have our wedding, won't they? Just like she said. Don't you think we should concentrate on *that*?"

"Yes, dear, I suppose you have a point. Does anyone have any ideas?"

"We could bang on the door and shout for help," Sayley suggested.

"And what if Leni hears us?" Lenora said. "She'd probably imagine us with no mouths."

"In fact," Coren reminded them all, "Cori could be listening to us right now. He eavesdropped last time." He thought some particular vicious thoughts in Cori's direction, just in case.

"That's not right," Milda stated. "Listening in on someone like that."

"Mother!" Coren objected. "I can't believe you're saying that. You listen in on my thoughts uninvited all the time."

"That's different, Coren dear," Milda answered. "You're my son. I have a right to do that. All mothers do."

Coren sighed and shook his head—it was going to be a very long eternity. He turned to Lenora. "What are we going to do?"

"For once," she replied, "I honestly can't think of a thing. I think we need to wish as hard as we can that someone discovers us."

*I couldn't possibly*, Coren thought to himself, *be wishing harder.*

Just then, the door to the closet opened. And standing in the doorway, looking through the bars, was—

"Michael!" Sayley cried. She pushed everyone aside and grasped the bars. "What on earth? How did you get here?"

"I'm . . . I'm not sure," he said. "I was imagining that you were in trouble, you know, because the way you described her, that Leni sounded very dangerous to me, and I was worried about what she might do. And I remembered this book I've been reading for school—it tells about how in ancient Greek plays a god often suddenly appears and saves everyone from whatever terrible trouble they're in. They call it a *deus ex machina*. And"—his cheeks grew red and he looked flustered—"well, I thought that it would be wonderful if *I* could do that. Me, little old Michael Amberson. Be a *deus ex machina*, I mean— suddenly appear and save everyone, like a superhero, you know? And then—well, I don't know exactly what happened then, but something did. Suddenly I was standing here in this corridor! And I heard voices coming from in here, so I opened the door and it looks like you really do need saving!"

"I don't understand," said Lenora. "When we were in Winnipeg, Michael couldn't imagine us out—how come he could imagine *himself* here?"

"It must be the combination of our wishing *plus* Michael's imagination that allowed him to do it," said Coren. "Good for you, Michael."

"Cool." Michael grinned.

"It's not cool in here at all, young man," King Arno said. "In fact, it's beginning to feel like we're in one of my cook ovens. Whoever you are, less talking and more action. Let us out."

Michael looked confused. "I can't. That is, I don't have a key."

Lenora's smile faded. "Of course," she said sadly. "A key. Leni probably didn't even imagine one into existence." She looked at Coren, slowly shaking her head. "Any ideas, Coren?" she said. "Please?"

"Well," he began, "actually I can't—"

"If you have any," she quickly interrupted, "tell us, but think about . . . oh, I don't know . . . orange sherbet while you're doing it."

"Orange sherbet? What?"

"If Cori is going to eavesdrop, Coren, we don't want him to hear our plans. So think about orange sherbet. In fact, all of you think about orange sherbet. I am." *Orange sherbet.*

*Orange sherbet,* thought Coren. *Got it.* "But actually, Lenora, without a key—" His face fell. "We're toast. Or orange sherbet."

"Blast," said Lenora. *Orange sherbet.* "Well, Michael, I guess we'll have to take a chance on sending you out there"—*orange sherbet*—"and hope that Leni and Cori don't notice you." *Orange sherbet.*

"You'll have to go look for Agneth," Coren instructed him. "He's the Keeper of the Balance, and if you could manage to get to him, then maybe—"

"No wait, Coren," exclaimed Lenora. *Orange sherbet!* "Michael!" *Orange sherbet.* "He can do it himself!" *Orange sherbet.* "Michael had the power to imagine himself here, right?" *Orange sherbet.* "If he could do that"—*orange sherbet*—"then—"

"Then," Coren continued, "he can imagine us out of here." *Orange sherbet!* "Do you think he could, Sayley?"

"I . . . I suppose so," she said. "I did want him to be able to imagine things, after all." *Lemon ice.* Sayley hated orange sherbet.

"Michael," said Coren. *Orange sherbet.* "I think you *could* get us out of here." *Orange sherbet.* "You can't give us our powers back—that would probably be too much—but I'll bet you can do this." *Orange sherbet.* "Look at this lock. And simply imagine that it is open!" *Orange sherbet.*

"That's it? Just imagine it?"

"Yes." *Orange sherbet.* "With all your strength. Imagine it isn't locked—it's open." *Orange sherbet.*

"Okay," said Michael. "Here goes." He closed his eyes.

A dish of orange sherbet suddenly appeared in the air in front of his face, then went crashing to the floor.

"A broom!" Queen Savet wailed. "I want a broom!"

"Not quite right, Michael," said Lenora. "But at least we know for sure that he can do it! Terrific, Michael—excellent for a beginner! Try again, and this time, everyone else just stop thinking for a while."

Michael closed his eyes.

When he opened them, the lock was gone. The iron gate was beginning to swing open.

## Chapter 24

"Bravo," said Lenora. "I knew you could do it! Isn't he wonderful, Sayley?"

Sayley blushed bright red.

"Good lad," said King Rayden. "I may have to give you a medal. I *will* give you a medal. In fact, I'll give you *lots* of medals."

"And I," King Arno added, "am going to make you your own special batch of cinnamon buns! With raisins in them!"

Michael grinned, very pleased with himself. Sayley gazed adoringly at him, equally pleased. Once a person got over the embarrassment of it, well, maybe imagining him hadn't been such a bad idea after all. He had actually saved them not once, but twice! And the way everyone was looking at him and being ever so pleased sort of made up for all the trouble they had been giving her about creating the rest of Michael's world. Why, Lenora was actually hugging him!

Hugging him very tightly. Just who did Lenora think she was, anyway? Michael was *hers,* and Lenora could just keep her big paws off him. Lenora already had Coren, after all.

Her arm still draped over Michael's shoulder, Lenora turned to everyone. "I think the best thing for us to do is to try to get to someone with the power to imagine *our* powers back. Five or six Gepethians working together ought to do it."

"Or," her father said, "Agneth could do it by himself."

"I suppose he could," said Lenora, her spirits sinking. Agneth, the Keeper of the Balance, had finally recovered from the breakdown he'd suffered as a result of their last unfortunate adventure and was now in full control of his extensive powers. But of all the people who might least like Lenora to have her powers back, Agneth was the prime candidate—and she could just imagine what he'd say when he heard about all the trouble her creation, Leni, had caused. He'd never let her forget it, never. "Anyway," she continued, "I suggest we all split up, because if Leni sees us together, she may suspect that we've escaped. But if she sees just one of us, she'll assume it's the double she made. If she does, just act very compliant, say yes to everything, pretend to be the double, and hope she doesn't catch on, right? Try to corner any Gepethians you see—quietly, of course—and get them to meet us back here in half an hour. And let's hope we get enough good minds together to make it work. Of course, Coren and I will have to stay out of her way completely."

"Or," her father added, "we might just find Agneth." Lenora pretended not to hear him.

"Good thinking, Lenora," said Milda. "Let's get moving. I want my thoughts back as quickly as possible. I have a lovely idea for a musical waterfall." She bustled past Lenora and Michael, humming.

"And don't forget, Mother," Coren called after her, "if

you happen to get anywhere near Cori, think about orange sherbet."

"Or lemon ice," said Sayley. "That's what *we're* thinking about, isn't it, Michael?" She grabbed his hand and pulled him away from Lenora and out into the hallway.

Soon Lenora was out there also, sneaking off toward the west wing, where all the Gepethian courtiers were staying. Not only was she most likely to find people with powerful imaginations there, but it was exactly in the opposite direction from the library, where, Lenora had noticed, the Keeper Agneth had taken to sitting with Kaylor, the Andillan Thoughtwatcher, going over the old records. She supposed Coren would head there to look for him, but with any luck Agneth would be out on one of his interminable walks around the courtyard, and she'd have gathered the powerful minds and done the job before he even returned. Then, with her imagination back—well, Agneth wasn't going to be pushing her around if she could possibly help it.

Lenora was about to turn the corner into the hallway where the Gepethians were staying when she heard a voice.

"Oh, Agneth, you are *so* clever," it gushed.

*Oh, no,* thought Lenora. Just how unlucky could a person get? It was Leni—and it seemed that she was talking to Agneth, of all people. Lenora flattened herself against the wall and listened.

"The wedding ceremony you've arranged is going to be perfect, Agneth. Simply perfect! I can't wait." And Lenora heard what distinctly sounded like a kiss.

Leni kissing that dried-up old bean? And of course he'd think it was her, Lenora herself. It was disgusting.

Now Lenora could hear Leni's footsteps heading off down the corridor—in the other direction, thankfully. She gave Agneth enough time to step back into his room and close the door, and then stepped into the corridor.

"Lenora, my dear!" said Agneth, who had been leaning against the door with a dreamy look on his face. "Back again so soon?"

Oh, no! The very thing she did not want.

Well, it was too late now. Her father would never forgive her if he learned she had actually found Agneth and not told him about the mess they were all in. She sighed deeply and walked toward him.

"Brace yourself, Agneth," she said. "I have some bad news for you."

"You do?" For a moment he just gazed into her face. "Of course," he said finally in a sad, small voice. "I should have known it. That wasn't you, was it? That wonderful, sensible, compliant person who was interested in nothing but pew ribbons and chants of celebration—it wasn't you at all."

"No, Agneth," said Lenora. "I'm afraid it wasn't. It was Leni—my double, remember? And even worse, she—"

"In my heart of hearts, I suppose, I knew it all along. I mean, I was actually beginning to *like* you. You kissed me! You, my nemesis, the Princess Lenora! Everything was going so smoothly. I should have known something was wrong."

"You bet there's something wrong," said Lenora, doing her best to ignore all the insults. "Leni stole my powers—and also, Mother's and Father's and Coren's and King Arno's and Queen Milda's and Sayley's!" Quickly, she filled him in on what had been happening all day.

For a moment after she finished he just shook his head. "You actually expect me to believe that sweet girl would do all that? Why, she's kind and gentle, like a properly balanced woman should be. She'd never hurt a fly."

"But she did, this time. She really did. You have to believe me, Agneth! You have to give me my powers back, or she'll get rid of me completely!"

A strange smile appeared on his face. "Tempting," he said, rubbing his chin thoughtfully. "Very tempting."

"Agneth," said Lenora, shocked. "You can't be serious! I *am* a princess, after all!" A thought suddenly occurred to her. "Besides which, you surely couldn't let her take away powers I'm *supposed* to have, could you? I mean, wouldn't that affect the—"

"The Balance," Agneth agreed, nodding his head glumly. "You're right, Lenora. Of course you're right. If I wish to do my duty as the Keeper and preserve the Balance, then I have to restore the power of the one person most likely to use that power to upset the Balance."

"Yes! You do!"

"Sometimes, you know, I wonder about this world we live in. Whoever or whatever created it must have a particularly bizarre sense of humor. It's enough to make a person just want to throw caution to the wind forever and spend the entire rest of his life hopping around on one leg."

*Oh, no,* thought Lenora, *not hopping!* During her last unfortunate adventure, the Keeper had hopped around on one leg for weeks, being deliberately *un*balanced, immersed in a fog of uncomprehending irrationality. If he started doing that again, she'd never get her powers back.

"But," said the Keeper, "duty is duty. There you are, Lenora— I've done it. You're back to normal. All I ask is that the next time you decide to get us all into terrible trouble, do keep me out of it. Put me into a deep sleep until it's over. I'm too old for all this, I tell you, too old."

As a test Lenora imagined she had something in her hand. She did—a dish of orange sherbet.

"You're wonderful, Agneth," she said, and kissed him on the cheek, just to confuse him. "I can deal with the rest of them, and you look like you could use some refreshment. Take this." Handing him the dish of sherbet, she left him stuttering something in a confused voice and swiftly headed back to find the others.

## Chapter 25

Coren was waiting for her. "I couldn't find—" He hadn't completed his sentence before he could hear Lenora's thoughts.

"Lenora!" he said, quite scandalized. "We're not even married!"

She threw her arms around him and gave him a big kiss. "But we will be soon," she said. "Now—what do we do about Leni?"

"I suggest we find our parents first and you can give them back their powers, too," Coren said. "Then we'll all decide."

It took them a while to round everyone up, including Sayley and Michael, but finally they were all together. Coren had decided to bring them all to the little meeting room just behind the throne room—a good place to talk where they were not likely to be seen.

"We must be on guard this time," King Rayden said. "We must all imagine that we *can't* be plucked of our powers, even if Leni does it suddenly."

They all did so—and just in time, for Leni bounced into the room, followed by Cori.

"Ah!" she said. "Good, you're all here, my servile clones. We have to talk!"

"Yes," said Lenora. "We do have to talk."

But just then another King Arno, Queen Milda, King Rayden, and Queen Savet entered.

"You summoned us, Leni," the new Queen Milda said meekly.

"We are here," said the new King Arno, "to do your bidding, Your Supreme Mightiness, without any foolish talk about cinnamon buns or any other baked goods."

Leni looked from one set of monarchs to the other.

"Uh-oh!" she said, and she immediately imagined the real monarchs tied in chains, with no powers. Coren could hear her think it.

"It won't work, Leni," Coren said.

"And that was *very* bad behavior," Queen Milda said.

"Oh dear!" said the other Queen Milda, horrified. "Oh dear, oh dear! How can you talk to the adorable, well-groomed Leni like that!"

"Yes," the duplicate King Arno agreed. "You need to have your mouth washed out with soap."

"This is outrageous," the real King Arno said. "I don't care how handsome and kingly you are, mister—you can't talk to my wife like that!"

"We are obviously going to have to punish you, Leni," said the real King Rayden. "Why, if it hadn't been for this boy . . ." He pointed at Michael.

"Yes," said Lenora. "You have wonderful powers, Michael, considering you didn't even know you had them."

Michael blushed and smiled shyly at her.

"No!" Coren shouted. "Don't do it, Leni!"

"What?" said Lenora.

"She was just about to turn Michael into a tree and plant him somewhere deep in the forests of Kirtznoldia."

Michael looked stricken. "No!" he exclaimed, but he glanced at his fingers, and they were indeed beginning to look more like twigs than fingers. "No! Oh, I wish you were just a puddle of *nothing*, like the Wicked Witch of the West—you and Cori and all your stupid doubles!"

Suddenly Leni began to melt. "Stop it!" she screamed. "I'm melting! I'm melting!"

Cori screamed and lunged at Michael with his sword, but his arm quickly turned liquid and he began to melt, too. Within seconds all that was left of Leni and Cori and the four fake monarchs was puddles on the ground.

Michael stared at the puddles in horror, as did everyone else. "But," said Michael, "I didn't mean . . . I . . . I've killed them!"

For a moment there was nothing but shocked silence. Then, almost imperceptibly, the surface of one of the puddles—the one that had been Leni—began to move, as if an invisible hand were stirring it. Circles appeared, expanding outward. First slowly, and then faster and faster, the puddle spun like a minia-ture whirlpool. Soon a figure began to grow out of the whirlpool, small to begin with, then becoming larger as it whirled along with the puddle beneath it.

Lenora was relieved. Leni had done some nasty things, but dissolving into nothingness like that was a worse punishment than even she deserved—besides which, Michael was terribly upset by the unexpected fulfillment of his wishes. Better to have Leni bring herself and the rest back than have the poor boy suffer. They could all figure out some more appropriate punishment for Leni and Cori later.

Except for one thing. The figure growing out of the puddle was *not* Leni. It was a man—a tall, handsome man with broad shoulders, curly black hair, and dazzling blue eyes.

It was Hevak. Her old enemy, Hevak, back again.

"So, Lenora," Hevak said, looking down at her with a wry half smile, "we meet again."

*Hevak*, thought Coren. *Of course. The malicious treatment they'd been receiving had seemed so uncharacteristic of Leni. It made much more sense if the powerful and very willful Hevak was involved. But just how, exactly, was he involved? Where had he come from, and how had he got there in the first place?*

There was no time to think about that now. The presence of Hevak in the room meant they were all in danger—serious danger. Coren steeled himself and prepared for the worst.

Lenora, meanwhile, was returning Hevak's smile. "I should have know it was you," she said. "Have you been there inside Leni's mind all along?"

"I'm afraid so," he said. "And let me tell you, it's a narrow little place in there—filled with ruffles and frills and furbelows. I hardly had any room to think, let alone imagine anything worthwhile—assuming, of course, that thinking ever *is* worthwhile. I apologize if the torture I put you through has disappointed you in any way."

"That's quite all right," said Lenora, a grim look on her face. "It's been tortuous enough, thank you very much."

As this conversation had been happening everyone else in the room had been staring at Hevak in shocked incomprehension. Who was he? And where had he come from?

"Lenora," said King Rayden, finally recovered enough from his shock to speak. "Who *is* this person?"

"Yes, who?" echoed Sayley.

"And," added Queen Savet, "why is he dripping water onto Milda's nice clean floors?"

Hevak turned and looked at her, apparently noticing the crowd gathered around him and Lenora for the first time.

"Sorry, Your Majesty," he said, immediately imagining himself and the floor under him dry. "But I want to talk to Lenora, not you—not any of you. For all your insignificance, you are distracting. Please be quiet."

Coren was about to tell Hevak to be quiet himself—but he couldn't. His lips would not move, no matter how hard he tried to move them. And, he could see, everyone else in the room was in the same situation. Despite their powers, furthermore, the Gepethians were no more able to do anything about it than the rest of them. Hevak had made sure that everyone but himself and Lenora would be just as quiet as he wanted them to be.

It was very worrying. If Hevak could do that and make it stick, it meant his powers were stronger than King Rayden's or Queen Savet's or even Sayley's. But, Coren told himself, surely Hevak wasn't more powerful than Lenora? Lenora would soon have everyone talking again and imagining again, and then the Gepethians could all work together to do something about

Hevak. Coren turned his immobilized face toward Lenora, willing her to act quickly.

But she didn't. Instead, she nodded at Hevak.

"This time, Hevak, I think you're right. This is between the two of us—I suppose it's always been between the two of us, hasn't it? Or at least, the two of us and Coren. And you know"—she gazed calmly into Hevak's steely blue eyes—"I am beginning to get very tired of you. It seems that every time I turn around you're there again, interfering with my life, spoiling my plans. It's unfair to everyone, including me. I can't take any more of it—and I won't. This time, I am simply going to have to imagine you into complete and utter nonexistence."

For a while Hevak just stared at her. "I suppose you are," he finally said with a huge sigh. "Which means, of course, that I will have to do the same to you, for such are the ways of the world. And I, of course, will win, Lenora, for no one's mind is stronger than mine—not even yours. I'll miss you, I suppose, but what has to be has to be. We might as well get started."

Remembering Lenora's earlier encounters with Hevak, Coren felt a sharp twinge of terror. Any minute now they might be surrounded by troops of angry white bears with sharp claws, or perhaps flames might begin to rain down out of the skies, right through the roof of the castle, and set their skin and clothing on fire and burn them all to a crisp.

*Or even better,* a thought crossed his mind, *the fire could rain up, out of the floor, and catch Hevak unawares. And then, maybe, a few carefully placed bombs? Or perhaps I'll just twist him up into a pretzel shape and make monkeys with long fingernails climb on him and tickle him to death.*

It was Lenora's thought. She was concentrating so hard on her plans for battling Hevak that Coren had caught what she was thinking without any conscious attempt to do so—which meant that Hevak had not deprived Coren of *his* powers. *Probably thinks I'm too inconsequential to even worry about,* Coren told himself ruefully—Hevak had a history of thinking much less of Coren than Coren liked.

But in their past encounters Hevak's underestimation of Coren had cost him—cost him a lot, in fact. Maybe luck was on their side after all.

At the moment, it didn't feel like luck. Lenora's thoughts were so intense they pierced Coren's mind like a hot knife going through soft butter. It hurt to hear her think.

But the pain was worth it if it could help Lenora to win her battle. The opposite outcome was too awful to even think about. A world dominated by Hevak and his extravagant whims, a world doomed to uncontrolled chaos and mayhem. Worst of all, a world without Lenora. In other words, a world not worth living in. There was no alternative—Coren had to do whatever he could to help Lenora survive and win. He took a deep breath and set his mind to hear not only Lenora's thoughts, but also her enemy's. His presence in Lenora's mind might help to give her strength, or at least a little reassurance. But listening to Hevak was more important. If he could hear what Hevak was planning and somehow pass it on to Lenora before the monster actually acted on it, it might give Lenora the few seconds she needed to come up with a way of saving herself and everyone else.

*I could just manufacture an entire battalion of Security,* Lenora was thinking, *and then turn Hevak into a giant doughnut, and they'll gnaw him into nothingness. Or how about a huge snowstorm with that nauseating Portage Place music playing in it and beating remorselessly on his ears? Hevak certainly deserves a bit of his own medicine.*

Meanwhile, Hevak was also making plans. *I could do a hurricane,*

*I suppose*, Coren heard in his thoughts as the picture of Lenora's snowstorm still continued to rage painfully around them. *Hurricanes are always effective, especially if I put some sharp little metal needles with poisoned tips into the wind.* As Hevak imagined the needles an image of them zapping into Lenora at an incredibly rapid pace and causing her to faint and fall filled Coren's mind, blotting out the snowstorm

*Lenora!* he thought, *Armor! Cover yourself with armor! Now!*

But no armor appeared—no matter how much he willed her to hear his thoughts, she hadn't done it.

On the other hand, no hurricane had appeared either, and no needles. Why hadn't Hevak done as he'd been thinking? Coren tuned in on Hevak's thoughts once more.

*Hurricanes, needles,* he was thinking. *Been there. Done that. Even got tired of the T-shirt. How boring.*

*Oops,* thought Coren, *now he's going to imagine something even worse. Poor Lenora. Poor all of us.*

But as the picture of the hurricane faded from Hevak's mind, nothing replaced it. Quite literally nothing—it was just a void now, not white or black or even gray. No thoughts or images of any sort appeared in it. Just nothing.

Which was, Coren knew from his own experience, impossible. People talked about having an empty mind, about not thinking of anything. But there was always something there, a vague memory, perhaps, a bit of a perception of a smell or a taste in one's mouth, a consciousness of where one's arms or legs happened to be. A mind was never really empty.

And yet Hevak's was—quite utterly empty. It was like he was no longer there at all, that he had simply disappeared out of his own thoughts.

And then, as Lenora kept glaring at him, he was back again. A picture of Lenora slowly filled the gray emptiness of Hevak's mind—Lenora exactly as she stood before him, staring up into his eyes. Lenora, Coren found Hevak thinking, as an annoying little nuisance he'd much rather not have to deal with.

"Lenora," Hevak now said with another huge sigh, "do we really have to do this?"

Chapter 27

"What?" Lenora was so surprised by what Hevak was saying that the image in her mind of him being stung by a swarm of angry giant hornets suddenly disintegrated.

"I mean," Hevak continued, "what's the point, exactly?"

"The point," Lenora said, "is to save us all from you."

"Oh," said Hevak, nodding. "I understand. You think I'm dangerous."

"Of course I do. You *are* dangerous."

"Well, I can certainly see where you would get that idea. I *have* caused you the occasional bit of trouble in the past, no doubt about it. And I could certainly do it again, if I wanted to. But the thing is—well, to tell the truth, Lenora, I don't want to."

She stared at him in disbelief. "'Don't want to'?"

"Don't want to. I mean, it all seems so silly, so pointless. What would it accomplish? It would cause a cataclysmic, earth-shattering disaster and make a terrible mess—your poor old mother would find that a few puddles on the floor were the least of her cleaning problems. And what would be the result of it all, besides all that turmoil and strife and disaster and mess? I would win, of course. Or, okay, I suppose for the sake of argument, it's even barely possible that you might win. One or the other—and the one who lost would no longer exist, and the one who won would get to do whatever he or she pleased. And the world would go on, more or less as it always has and always will. Why even bother?"

"But . . . but . . ." Lenora was too flabbergasted to know what to say.

"Oh, yes," Hevak continued. "I know. You think I *want* to do as I please. And I do, I suppose. But the thing is, it turns out that what I want to do is as little as possible. I'm tired of interfering with the way things are. I tried to make everything exactly the way I thought it should be back when I was running the country of Grag, and what happened? Everyone called me evil. After that, when I landed in the reverse world and tried to be good, it was never good enough. Nobody was ever satisfied. What was the point of even trying? I've experienced evil, Lenora, and I've experienced good—and I tell you, I'm tired of them both. I'm beyond good and evil. And to make matters worse, living in Leni's mind has worn me out altogether. I am exhausted. I don't want to fight you, although of course I will if you insist—and most likely win, I suppose, as if it matters. But really all I want is to be left alone. I want to be free to empty my mind and contemplate the emptiness of existence."

*Well,* Coren thought, *he certainly did know how to empty his mind—he'd just been seeing the evidence. Was it possible that Hevak was actually telling the truth?*

Lenora, meanwhile, was wondering the exact same thing. Hevak seemed sincere—but then Hevak had always seemed sincere, just before he snuck up on her and did something totally outrageous. "What do you think, Coren," she asked. "Can we trust him?"

"Mmmph," said Coren.

"Oh, sorry, I forgot. There."

"Thanks," said Coren, his mouth working again. "I don't know, Lenora. I mean"—he took another careful dip into Hevak's mind, which now seemed to be surprisingly empty again—"his thoughts don't seem to be hiding anything—nothing at all, which is strange but not, I suppose, very dangerous. But then . . ." He turned to Hevak. "If you're so uninterested in fighting with Lenora, Hevak, then why did you do all this to us? Why did you put us in Winnipeg? Come to think of it, why are you here at all?"

"What?" Hevak started, as if awaking out of a trance. "Oh, that. It was really Leni's fault. She called me here."

"Called you?"

"Yes," Hevak continued. "And I doubt she even realized she was doing it. The poor, sad thing would never consciously do anything so Balance-shattering—I can't imagine what you were thinking of when you imagined her, Lenora. She's really beneath your skills. But when she saw all the attention you and this freckle-faced boy were getting because of your wedding, she got jealous. She got to thinking how much happier she'd been back when you and I were being so good to her—when we were giving her every hairdo she desired as soon as she desired it. She didn't know it was me and my goodness inside you making you do it, Lenora. But when she wished things could be that way again, she nevertheless called me out of the void I'd disappeared into and inside her mind to be with her. And I came."

*It made sense*, Coren thought. Being a duplicate, Leni shared Lenora's memories up to the time of her creation—including memories of the time when Hevak had been part of Lenora herself, an embodiment of Lenora's own wishes. He was, then, equally a part of Leni, bound to come when she called him back to her.

"I had to come," Hevak said, "much as I hated giving up the wonderful peace and quiet of my empty existence. And once I got here, I made things happen as she wanted, more or less. It just wasn't worth the trouble not to do it."

"More or less?" asked Lenora.

"Yes. Once I found myself inside her mind, I kept hearing her tell herself that of course she didn't want to change anything, but I could tell she really did. She wanted to be rid of you, and she wanted to be the center of attention herself. So I made her do what she actually wanted, despite her so-called better judgment. I got her to imagine you and your red-haired friend into the Winnipeg world, where you couldn't get yourselves out again, and I encouraged her to pretend to be you. It made her happy in spite of herself. Inside, deep down inside, she's still really you and me, Lenora—never so happy as when she's getting her own way."

Lenora gave him an angry look.

"Anyway," he continued, "it quieted her down and gave me time to think. To think of the wonderful meaningless nothingness of it all! You can't begin to imagine how wonderful it is to think of nothing. It's so totally and completely uninteresting!"

Coren, in fact, caught him doing it—for a brief instant Hevak's mind was empty again, and then, as he remembered where he was, it filled with the desire for emptiness.

"What I don't understand," Coren said, "is why you didn't just extinguish us altogether. Why keep us alive at all?"

"Oh," said Hevak, "I don't know. I suppose I just couldn't bring myself to do it. Think about it. In the long run, in the scheme of things, what difference does it make if you live or die? Or if I do, for that matter, or anybody ever at all? And if it doesn't make any difference, then why bother to do anything about it? For that matter, why bother doing anything? What would be the point? On the other hand, of course, what would be the point of *not* doing it? It makes you stop and think, doesn't it? It makes you stop and think for a long, long time."

*Yes,* thought Coren, *if you felt like that, it would certainly make you stop and think—for a very long time. You might never get around to deciding to do anything. You might end up doing nothing and, eventually, thinking nothing.*

Just as Hevak seemed to be doing. "He seems sincere, Lenora," said Coren. "I think we have to trust him."

"I suppose," said Lenora, "that I really didn't want to get rid of him for good. In a strange way it'd be like cutting off an arm or a leg. But we can't simply let him go—it's too dangerous."

"No, I promise you," said Hevak, "it isn't. All I want to do is go back into nothingness. I'm going there right now." Once more Coren could feel Hevak's mind recede. Indeed, even his body seemed to thin out a little, as if it, too, were beginning to vanish.

"No, Lenora," said Coren. "Don't let him go." It seemed too dangerous to let Hevak do what he wanted.

Lenora willed him to stay. He did. "Whatever you say, Lenora." Hevak sighed. "What difference does it make, really?"

"You're right, Coren," she said. "Who knows when he might get over this strange mood and decide that something or other—who knows what?—is better than nothing. We can't take a chance on that. But what else can we do with him?"

"Mmphl-bmph," a voice said. It was Michael, gesturing earnestly to attract their attention. He and the rest were still as immobile as Hevak had imagined them, and unable to talk.

"What is it, Michael?" asked Lenora, imagining he could

answer her. At the same time, she imagined the rest of them back to normal, too.

"I hope you don't mind," said Michael, "but being stuck here like that, I really had no choice but to eavesdrop on your conversation—and I have an idea. The thing is, back home in Winnipeg I know a lot of people who just like to hang around and think nothing and imagine nothing and do nothing. My school is full of them, and so is the city council. This guy"—he gestured toward Hevak—"would fit right in there."

"Of course!" Lenora said. "Michael, you're a genius! We'll put Hevak in Winnipeg! Nobody has any imagination there, so he wouldn't feel out of place. And he wouldn't be able to use his own imagination to get out again, so we'd all be safe from him, and so would all the Winnipeggers."

"I wouldn't be able to use my imagination?" said Hevak. "I wouldn't be able to change the course of events or make anything different happen? I'd be stuck with things exactly as they are?"

"Of course," said Lenora. "You've seen Sayley's awful world. You know what it's like."

"Yes," he said. "Yes, I do. It's awful—the perfect place to remind me of the pointlessness of life. It sounds wonderful—even more meaningless than nothing at all. Please do send me there, Lenora—if you wish to, of course, or more accurately, if fate decides you will. One way or the other. It really doesn't matter."

But Lenora could see it did matter. Hevak wanted to go to Winnipeg.

But he didn't know, really, what he was getting into. Lenora shuddered, remembering her experiences there. "We'll send him there," she said. "But Sayley, you must change it as soon as the final judging is over. It really isn't fair to leave Hevak and all the rest of those people living like that forever. Even Hevak doesn't deserve that much punishment, even if he thinks he wants it. It's just too cruel."

"I suppose so," said Sayley. "Although it does seem a pity to spoil it."

"I'd feel better about it," Lenora urged, "if you made it even a *little* nicer."

"I know!" Sayley declared. "What I'll do is I'll make it bigger! I'll invent its history, and I'll give everybody memories of their childhood! I'll make it into a whole world, with mountains and valleys and oceans and other cities! And the other cities will have *outdoor* rocks to climb and they won't have snow all the time, so if anybody gets tired of Winnipeg they'll be able to go somewhere different! But—oh, this is so good!—but nobody will ever want to go anywhere else! Because the people in Winnipeg all love Winnipeg so much, right, they'll think the other better places are horrible, and they'll *want* to stay in Winnipeg. They'll think it's the best place there is! Is that nice enough for you, Lenora?"

"Well," Lenora mused, "it isn't exactly what I . . ." She turned to Michael. "You have to live there. Anything *you'd* like changed?"

"Not really," he said. "I *love* Winnipeg."

"See?" said Sayley, smiling triumphantly.

"It would be nice, I guess," Michael added, "if there could be an *actual* summer."

"Oh, there will be," Sayley assured him. "But it still has to be the worst place, right? I don't want to spoil it, even if it is a little nicer. So in summer I'll put in, I don't know, some bugs, maybe. Yes, bugs! Monstrous-looking insects called mosquitoes that will buzz around everybody all summer long. And they'll . . . they'll suck your *blood*!"

"Sayley!" Lenora scolded.

"That's all right," Michael said, puffing out his chest. "We Winnipeggers are tough. We won't be afraid of any blood-sucking insects. We can handle *anything*!"

"Handle anything, eh?" Sayley said. "Just wait till you see the cankerworms! Thousands of wiggly green worms that'll hang down from the trees every summer and get in your hair and everywhere!"

"Cool," said Michael.

"Very cool," Sayley nodded. "Now, let's go see the exhibits, Michael—maybe I'll get a few more good ideas for Winnipeg. I haven't figured out what happens between winter and summer yet, and there's a mud world I want a closer look at, where everybody's shoes stick into the ground all the time."

"Or," said Michael, "how about a flood? The river could get very high, and . . ."

"Of course!" Sayley said. "Michael, you're a genius!"

As Sayley and Michael walked off down the hall, deep in discussion, Lenora turned to Hevak. "Are you ready?" she said.

"Yes," he said. "Not that it really matters. But I am ready."

"Then," said Lenora, "the time has come to say good-bye. Good-bye, Hevak. Good-bye, with any luck, forever. I hope Winnipeg is everything you hope for."

"Thank you, Lenora. Good-bye." He began, once more, to thin out as Lenora concentrated on him not being there—she was imagining him in Portage Place, near the ugly clock. Soon Coren could see right through him.

"I hope, Lenora," Hevak said in a surprisingly firm voice just before he disappeared altogether, "I hope that the rest of *your* life is everything *you* might hope for. I hope it's perfect, completely and totally perfect."

## Epilogue

*Funny*, thought Lenora as she stood at the back of the chapel waiting for the first notes of her processional music to begin. *I spent all that time getting mad at Leni and belittling her obsession with pew ribbons and styles of wedding dresses, but it turned out to be a good thing after all.*

A very good thing. The chapel looked wonderful, and so did her wedding dress. Everything was perfect—and she had Leni to thank for it.

In fact, Lenora realized, she couldn't have survived the wedding preparations without Leni. When Coren had first insisted that she bring Leni back from nonexistence, she had objected—good riddance, she thought. But after Coren reminded her that their awful time in Winnipeg hadn't actually been Leni's fault, she really didn't see that she had much choice about it. Or about Cori either—even though Coren wasn't quite so insistent about it, she brought back Cori, too.

As it turned out, once Leni returned and no longer had

Hevak controlling her mind, she was completely mortified by the part she'd played in recent events. She was so pathetically apologetic that Lenora had decided to try to cheer her up by making Leni her maid of honor and putting her in charge of the wedding arrangements—after all, she'd already made most of them.

And no question about it, she'd done a wonderful job—and she was being a wonderful and wonderfully supportive maid of honor. No, Lenora told herself, Leni wasn't such a bad person once you got to know her—she was turning out to be a good friend. Leni stood now at the front of the chapel, her dress almost as lovely as Lenora's own, looking very pleased with the work she had done—and so she should. Cori, standing on the other side of the altar in his role as best man, couldn't take his eyes off her.

Lenora was beginning to change her mind about Cori, too. He had a surprisingly soft heart buried under all that bluster, and Lenora's new willingness to befriend his beloved Leni had allowed him to show it to her on more than one occasion. She was beginning to see what Leni saw in Cori. And he certainly could do wonders with a dragon.

All things considered, Lenora was glad that Coren was spending more time with his double. Coren needed a friend, too—and maybe some of that courage of Cori's would wear off on him, and he'd turn out to be an even more perfect husband than he was going to be already. Although, come to think of it, that was hard to imagine. Coren was just right.

Completely right, she told herself as she watched him enter through the side door, looking adorable in his outfit of powder blue. He moved to stand beside Cori by the altar as the music continued to play.

It was turning out to be a dream of a wedding. The chapel

decorations were spectacular but tasteful, and everyone looked wonderful in their wedding outfits, even Agneth, who stood by the ceremonial pool at the front, firmly planted on both legs and looking very elegant in his ritual robes.

And now the bridal music began—the beautiful, swelling melody Leni had selected for her to march to. Lenora started down the aisle, returning the wide smile that Coren beamed at her.

*Lenora has never looked more lovely*, thought Coren as he watched her move slowly toward him in time with the music, her face radiating the joy they both felt. *I must be the luckiest person in all the worlds. Everything is just about perfect.*

And soon it would be absolutely perfect. Soon Agneth would complete the water sanctification that represented the meeting and blending of their two minds and hearts by having them gaze together into the pool. At that moment the new world would be born, the wonderful world Lenora herself had imagined and entered into the Meeting of Minds contest.

No question about it, thought Coren, Lenora deserved to win the contest. Life was going to be better now for everybody in all the worlds. Things would be perfect.

Too perfect, Coren suddenly found himself thinking—a niggling little thought at the back of his mind, hardly noticeable in the midst of all the happiness.

Where had that ridiculous thought come from? He and Lenora were deliriously happy with each other and just moments away from finally being married. Hevak was gone, surely gone for good this time—and a marvelous new world was about to be born. There was no reason to believe that they and everyone else were not going to live happily ever after.

And yet, he realized, that was exactly what was bothering him. It was too happy, somehow. It seemed—well, unnatural. A sort of dream world that could come to an end at any time.

*Don't be silly,* he told himself as Lenora came up to him and took his hand, beaming even more joyfully than before. *Don't be such a ridiculous worrywart.* If Lenora ever found out he was thinking such stupidly negative thoughts, she'd tease him remorselessly. And so she should. There was nothing to worry about now, absolutely nothing. From now on their lives were going to be everything they might wish for. They were going to be perfect, completely and totally perfect.

He beamed back at Lenora as they turned toward Agneth. The moment had arrived. Agneth smiled and beckoned them to turn their gaze downward into the pool.

"As the waters blend and balance in their flawless fluidity," said Agneth, "so shall you, Lenora of Gepeth, and you, Coren of Andilla, meet in a marriage of true minds and be a balance to each other. Merge now, now and forever, as your images merge in the waters, and be as one and perfect. Move forward, my children, and observe your future."

Eagerly anticipating their future together, Lenora and Coren looked into the pool.